The Pattern of Piney Series

STITCHED by Memory

BOOK TWO

By Katharine E. Hamilton

ISBN-13: 979-8-9856240-6-9

Stitched By Memory
The Pattern of Piney Series
Book Two

www.katharinehamilton.com

Cover Design by Kerry Prater.

"You have a place in my heart that no one else ever could have."

F. Scott Fitzgerald

All Titles
By Katharine E. Hamilton

The Brothers of Hastings Ranch Series
Graham
Calvin
Philip
Lawrence
Hayes
Clint
Seth

The Siblings O'Rifcan Series
Claron
Riley
Layla
Chloe
Murphy
Sidna

The Lighthearted Collection
Chicago's Best
Montgomery House
Beautiful Fury
Blind Date
McCarthy Road
Heart's Love

The Unfading Lands Series
The Unfading Lands
Darkness Divided
Redemption Rising

A Love For All Seasons Series
Summer's Catch
Autumn's Fall

The Pattern of Piney Series
Hooked By Love
Stitched By Memory
Brushed By Hope

Mary & Bright: A Sweet Christmas Romance

Captain Cornfield and Diamondy the Bad Guy Series
Great Diamond Heist, Book One
The Dino Egg Disaster, Book Two

The Adventurous Life of Laura Bell
Susie At Your Service
Sissy and Kat

Chapter One

"*Now, you eat all* your vegetables, Reesa. Clare picked those straight from Theo's garden. We can't let her hard work go to waste." Billy Lou Whitley smiled in encouragement across her dinner table.

Theodore Whitley snickered at his girlfriend's displeasure in eating the roasted carrots on her plate as she nudged them from one side to the other.

"Come on, Mom," her daughter, Clare, chimed in. "They'll improve your eyesight."

"My eyesight is fine, thank you very much," Reesa mumbled and then looked to Theo. "It's not that I don't like carrots, it's just—"

"That having them at every meal for two weeks is starting to make them less appetizing," he finished for her, and she nodded. "I hear ya. Time to start canning, Grandma." Theo smirked at Billy Lou as he took the last bite of his own carrot serving. "I'm a bit burned out too."

Relief washed over Billy Lou's face. "About time, Theodore. I was just waiting for the word from you that I could go over to that garden of yours and dig the rest of them up. You know how hard it's been trying to come up with new ways of using carrots? I was even mixing them in spaghetti sauce the other night just to use some up. And I made such a large helping of chuckwagon carrots for the church social last week that the bottom of the foil pan almost fell out as I walked them into the fellowship hall. I'm telling ya, it's a blessing, but it's also been a struggle to get creative. I'll head over tomorrow and dig the rest up."

"I'll help," Clare offered, her newfound joy in gardening creating a fun opportunity for her and Theo to spend time together.

"Wonderful." Billy Lou looked at Reesa and she smiled.

"That's all you and Clare this go around. I'm working on a new pattern for my website and am in the midst of prepping it for release," Reesa replied. Her crochet business still a steady stream of income for her and her daughter and one of the reasons she was able to move to Piney in the first place. Since her arrival, Piney didn't seem so quiet anymore, especially in Billy Lou's grandson's life. Theodore, despite his years of singleness, had fallen head over heels in love with the woman, and their budding relationship gave the small town a buzz of fresh gossip, interest, and excitement.

"How exciting!" Billy Lou couldn't wait. She loved Reesa's work. "I can't wait to see it."

A loud pop and sputter shot through the air from outside the house and had everyone jumping in their seats. Clare's eyes rounded and she immediately ducked closer to Theo. "What was that?"

Theo stood to his feet, Reesa grabbing his hand. "Don't go out there! Are you crazy? That sounded like a gun shot."

"No, it sounded like a car backfiring." He gently squeezed her hand. "I'll go take a look." As a mechanic, Theo knew the sound of vehicles well, and all three ladies relaxed in their seats once more.

"I can tell you right now who it is." Billy Lou rolled her eyes. "It's that man who lives over by the ol' Benson place, Charlie Edwards. Apparently, he's a car junkie and enthusiast. He's rattled on by in only God knows what for the last month since he's been here."

"I didn't realize there was a new person in town." Reesa leaned to peer out the window but didn't see anything.

"If you can call him new." Billy Lou began clearing plates. "Charlie went to school here in Piney. Born and raised. Then he took off after high school and no one ever really heard much about him. We knew he'd inherited his daddy's land, but he never came back to do anything with the place until recently."

"Interesting." Reesa and Clare gathered up the half-filled glasses and remaining dishware and carried them towards the sink. "When did he graduate high school?"

"Same year I did."

"Oh, so he's... older."

Billy Lou hooted. "You can say old, Reesa. It's not going to offend me." She patted the younger woman on the shoulder before turning back to the dishes. "Yes, he is. An old bachelor, too, from what I hear. Betty was giving me the scoop at the salon last week. From what she'd found out, he never married."

"That's kind of sad." Clare began loading the dishwasher without being asked and Billy Lou rubbed a gentle hand down her long, soft ponytail. She loved the sweet girl and her mom, and continually thanked the man upstairs for bringing them into her grandson's life. And into hers. "Not everyone is cut out for marriage. Best to understand that instead of tangling up in one and messing it up for years."

"Does he have any family nearby?" Reesa asked.

"Not that I'm aware. Most of them have died off or moved off. I haven't seen Charlie since graduation all those years ago. Granted, if he ever did come home to visit, I was lost in my own marriage and raising babies at the time." Billy Lou's soft smile of remembrance had her nudging Reesa's hip with her own. "You know how that is. Babies don't give you much free time to go out and about to socialize, especially in the early days."

"That is true." Reesa winked at her daughter. "Though Clare was pretty easygoing, thankfully."

"That's because I'm awesome." Clare smiled proudly, her cell phone buzzing on the counter. Her face warmed. "It's Teddy asking if I can go see a movie with a few friends. Is that okay?"

Reesa pondered the request for a moment.

"It's Friday night, Mom," Clare pointed out. "And it's only seven. I could probably be home by ten or ten-thirty."

"Eleven is fine," Reesa stated, and Clare excitedly shot a text back to her friend. *Friend* being a loaded word. Lately, Teddy Graham had been making more and more appearances in their lives and his intentions were that he was sweet on Clare. But the two were such good friends, Billy Lou wasn't sure if anything would develop beyond that or not unless the boy grew some gumption.

"He's going to pick me up from here," Clare replied. "Think he can get past Theo without the third degree?" She looked out the window at her mom's boyfriend talking with an older man, both standing over the open hood of an antique car. "Oh, cool! Look at his car!" Clare waved the other two women over. "It's super old."

"A street rod," Billy Lou replied. "Or hot rod, however you want to say it. A giant money pit might be better suited. Looks like he has his work cut out for him on that one."

"It's all rusty." Clare looked to Reesa. "Can I go see it?"

Her daughter's new love for vehicles since working at Theo's mechanic garage had the other woman agreeing. "If Theo seems annoyed with you coming out there, just wait on the porch for Teddy."

"Deal." Clare hugged Billy Lou. "See you tomorrow, Billy Lou."

Billy Lou relished the hug and gave the girl a loving squeeze. "Looking forward to it, honey." And she was out the front door and jogging across the yard towards Theo in a flash. Her grandson glanced up, and instead of his usual scowl, a look of pride washed over his face as he waved a hand towards her and introduced her to the older gentleman. Reesa and Billy Lou watched as they easily roped her into their conversation, and quickly had her headfirst inside the engine, poking around and looking at the antique vehicle.

Reesa chuckled. "Not sure Theo realized that by hiring Clare at the garage, he was hiring a prodigy. That girl has learned more about cars in the last month than she's ever learned about crafting. She has a knack for it, and that's saying something because she can crochet likes nobody's business."

"Oh, it's new and exciting. And she gets paid."

Reesa laughed. "Yeah, maybe that's why they're so appealing."

"She's a good one, Reesa. That's for certain. You both are. And look at Theodore... he adores her too."

Sighing, Reesa watched them interact. "He does, doesn't he? It makes my heart swell each time he shows kindness or sweetness to her. He's a good one, Billy Lou," she repeated her own words back at her and Billy Lou chuckled.
"He is, isn't he?" She winked at Reesa. "Now, do we go out there and act interested in their conversation or do we stay in here?"

"Have you spoken to Charlie since he's been back in town?"

"No, I haven't. Our paths haven't crossed yet."

"Well, I'd say they're crossing now." Reesa motioned towards his broken-down car blocking her driveway.

Billy Lou fluffed her hair and peered at her reflection in a small hall mirror.

"Are you primping, Billy Lou?" Reesa asked in amusement.

"Honey, that man hasn't seen me in over fifty years. You better believe I'm primping. I have a reputation to uphold."

Laughing, Reesa opened the front door and they both walked out to the now awaiting crowd. "He's handsome," Reesa whispered.

"He always was," Billy Lou added.

"And buff." Reesa's comment had Billy Lou turning in surprise. "What? He is. He's like a vintage Marlboro Man." She elbowed Billy Lou in the side.

"I don't know why you're nudging me." Billy Lou looked at the young woman in amusement. "I am old, romance is not on the agenda. Especially with Charlie Edwards, the fool."

"You are not old," Reesa contradicted. "You're beautiful, smart, sassy, and *the* ultimate catch."

"You're going to give me a big head if you keep on like that." Billy Lou grabbed Reesa's hand and tucked it into her elbow with a loving pat. "You're sweet to love me so, but Charlie Edwards has always been nothin' but trouble. And I don't like trouble."

"Well, it's been fifty years. Maybe things are different for him too," Reesa offered.

Doubtful, Billy Lou sighed. "Maybe so. Guess I should at least let him have a fresh start here in Piney. It's up to him whether or not it'll be a good one. But I'm going to make him earn it."

^

Theo looked up as Reesa and his grandmother traipsed up the driveway towards the road where he stood with Clare and the older gentleman whose rusty tin can of a vehicle had broken down.

"Mom, you have to see this truck. It's a Ford from 1932!" She all but squealed the last of her words and tugged Reesa forward and then pointed at her. "This is my mom, Reesa," Clare introduced. "Mom, this is Mr. Charlie. He restores old trucks and cars. Isn't that so cool? I told him about your love affair with Billy Lou's Corvette."

"Not *my* Corvette," Billy Lou huffed, extending her hand. "Billy Lou Whitley." It had been fifty years plus, but Charlie Edwards would have never forgotten Billy Lou Waldrup. And the woman looked just as beautiful seasoned with age as she did in her youth. He wondered if she was still as sassy.

"Charlie Edwards." He shook her hand and knew she recognized his name. "Pretty sure we went to school together back in the day. My daddy lived up the road for years after I left school."

"Ah, right." Billy Lou politely smiled and relinquished her hold on his hand.

"Sorry about this breaking down right in front of your pretty house." Charlie nudged the tire of the truck with his boot. "It's a new purchase. This was my first road test to see what all I would need to do to fix that engine up. Didn't know I'd be breaking down in front of a mechanic." He chuckled as Theo shrugged in acknowledgment. "I guess that's some good luck."

"Theodore is my grandson," Billy Lou stated.

"Grandson," Charlie repeated quietly. "Well, I'll be. Hard to believe Billy Lou Waldrup is all grown up and has grandkids. Good for you, Billy Lou. Good for you. I'd heard of Jerry's passing, I'm sorry about that. Truly. He was a good one."

Billy Lou's back stiffened at his words, but she nodded. "He was. Thank you."

"Well, I should get out of y'all's hair. I'm just going to implore your grandson for a ride back over to my place and I'll hitch up my trailer on my other truck and come pick this rust bucket up."

"What kind of truck do you drive on a regular basis?" Clare asked.

"Oh, nothing this old." Charlie chuckled. "Though maybe it would be considered old to a young cat like you."

"We're helping him right, Theo?"

Theo's face held an unreadable expression as he looked to the girl.

"It'd go quicker with more help," she continued. "*And* it's neighborly." She waved her hand over all the people that stood around.

"It's alright, sweetheart." Charlie laughed. "This isn't my first breakdown. I can manage on my own no problem."

"My truck can tow it back to your place and save you a trip," Theo offered in his typical way of no smile and no room for argument.

"Oh," Charlie's silver brows perked up. "Well, that would be right handy. Yeah, if you don't mind, that'd be great. I could get you to back her right into the garage for me." Thankful, Charlie shook Theo's hand. He seemed like a nice guy; a bit hard on the surface, but he held a softness for the girl and her mother which was evident in how his demeanor relaxed in their presence. Billy Lou stood quietly, observant, not attempting small talk. Was she upset with him? He couldn't tell. But she seemed aloof. And though they'd been in different social circles in high school, he only had fond memories of a fun, friendly, beautiful girl that would flash her pretty smile in genuine friendship but still have all the boys drooling after her. But this Billy Lou seemed almost like she was suspicious of him for some reason. "It was good to see you, Billy Lou. Would love to catch up one day and get the scoop on what's happened in Piney over all these years."

"I don't gossip, Charlie Edwards," Billy Lou quipped and had Reesa's brows slightly rising in surprise at her harsh tone.

Charlie looked her in the eye. "Well now, I didn't say you did, did I?" he challenged. "Just wondering what all I've missed in the last few decades."

"Then I guess you should have been here." Billy Lou waved her hand towards the women. "Come on, girls, we have dishes to take care of."

Clare's mouth opened with rebuttal, but Theo cast her a nod to follow her mother and Billy Lou and she did so in quiet resignation. When they were out of earshot, Charlie let out a low whistle. "She is still mad at me after all these years." He shook his head with a small smile. "Guess that means she remembers me, huh?" He looked at Theo and the man's eyes held his.

"Anything I need to be concerned about?"

Laughing, Charlie shook his head. "No sir. Your grandmother was quite the looker back in the day.

Still is from what I can see. Every boy in town was in love with Billy Lou. And I'll admit I was a bit smitten myself. So, one Friday night after the football game, I was hanging out under the bleachers with my buddies and Billy Lou comes waltzing by with the other cheerleaders. She dropped her little makeup bag and I bent to pick it up." Charlie looked up at Theo. "And that's when I planted one on her. A loud smack to her lips."

Theo's surprise was evident, and Charlie guffawed. "She slapped the tar out of me." He continued to laugh at the memory as her grandson did the same. "It was worth it, though. I was the envy of every male within a tri-county radius. After that, though, Billy Lou ignored me like the flea I was. I can see she might still hold a grudge. For weeks, people teased her about it. Some even started the rumor that we were sweet on one another. But by then, she and your granddaddy had started courtin'. You can see who won out in the end. Jerry was a good guy too. Were they happy?" he asked.

Theo nodded. "Yes."

"Good." Charlie nodded in appreciation. "Let's get this junk hooked up. I don't want to take any more of your time. I'm not blind when I see your interaction with the pretty brunette. I don't want to keep you from enjoying your time with her or her daughter."

"I'll get my keys." The front door of Billy Lou's house opened, and the young girl ran out again carrying the keys Theo had just mentioned.

"Mom said I could go if it was alright with you." She looked at Theo with hopeful eyes.

"That's fine. Load up." He tossed her the keys back and she squealed in excitement as she began backing the tow truck down the driveway and towards Charlie's old pickup. In surprising accuracy, she lined up the hitch with his front bumper and waited patiently for the men to do their work.

Chapter Two

Billy Lou sat in her usual spot at Java Jamie's, the cheerful red head and namesake bouncing with joy at the thought of a new person in town and one that seemed to know Billy Lou from her old days. Jamie didn't use the term "old days"— she was much too polite for that— but watching her face light up when Reesa explained how handsome Charlie Edwards was made Billy Lou feel as if she were in the lunchroom all over again. Part of her wanted to admit that she, too, thought Charlie had seasoned into quite an attractive man. But the other part of her felt guilty for even the thought. What would Jerry think if she gave into temptation and sat gushing over another man? Her heart broke a little at the depth of loss that accompanied her memories of

Jerry. He was supposed to still be here. Never had she given him permission to check out early. That was their deal; they'd pass on at the same time, enter the Lord's dwelling hand in hand, and never have to spend a day apart. Only, that's not what happened. Instead, Billy Lou was left with a Jerry-sized hole in her life that nothing or no one could ever fill except for an unsurmountable amount of grief that lingered under the surface. Oh, she was great at masking that emotion, but it stayed with her. Grief would never leave. She'd grown wise in knowing that it was just now a part of her and always would be. An unwanted friendship, for sure, but death was part of life. And she could still enjoy her own life and all its happy moments, but if she let her heart linger on the 'what ifs' or the 'I wishes,' she'd have days of digging herself out of that pit of melancholy and loss. It was better to think about the now, her new friends, and the new excitement in Theodore's life with Reesa and Clare. To watch her grandson fall in love was like watching crystals form: a beautiful, slow progression that resulted in something magnificent. Theo blossomed with Reesa, and the opposite could be said too. Both were growing comfortable with the fact that they were loved for who they are and not who they had been.

"I think Billy Lou needs to invite him for dinner one night." Jamie wriggled her eyebrows. "Catch up."

"Not going to happen, sweetie." Billy Lou took a sip

of her coffee, the robust flavor of roasted pecan adding a touch of sweetness to the bold grounds and helping wake her up with each taste.

"Clare liked him." Reesa continued to chat with Jamie. "She said he was funny and that even Theo laughed a couple of times."

Jamie's eyes darted to the door as the bell rang and she quieted. "Well, well, well," she whispered. "Is that him?" She hurried behind the counter and spread her arms in welcome. "Welcome to Java Jamie's. I'm Jamie. What can I get started for you, handsome?"

Charlie looked up at the menu board, his white hair a stark contrast to the grease smudges up and down his arms and clothes. He reached into his back pocket and withdrew his old leather wallet and unfolded it as he spoke. Billy Lou couldn't hear his conversation, but Jamie, in her usual way, had him smiling and laughing by the time she slid his cup across the counter. His smile dimmed slightly when it landed on Billy Lou and Reesa. It remained polite, but trepidation had it wavering as he approached. "Mornin', Billy Lou. Reesa, wasn't it?"

"Sure was." She patted the empty chair across from her. "Have a seat."

His eyes glanced at Billy Lou and taking her lack of response as a signal, he politely declined. "I wish I could, but I'm here for a quick pick-me-up before I head to your husband's garage."

Reesa's brows rose and Jamie squealed behind the counter before throwing her hands up like she was minding her own business. Reesa's cheeks blushed. "He's not my husband."

"Yet," Billy Lou and Jamie stated at the same time and Charlie smirked.

"My apologies. Well, your fella, then. He's graciously letting me bring in my new pickup to help me with a thorough comb through of what I'm going to need to do. I've given it one myself, but it always helps to have a true professional give it a once over before I start taking it apart."

"Wise of you," Billy Lou commented.

"Theo is the best," Reesa bragged. "And if he offered, jump on it. He doesn't usually do that. Oh… and while you're there, you should mention how handy it would be to have a car wash in town."

Billy Lou couldn't help the hoot of laughter that burst forth from her lips at Reesa's insistent plan to have Theodore start a local car wash in Piney. "You are relentless."

"Diversify, diversify, diversify. And save his girlfriend hours of work." Reesa shrugged. "Business sense, Billy Lou."

"My, my, my! Sounds like you're as formidable as Billy Lou." Charlie complimented. "No wonder you two get along. I'll see what I can do to help you out, sugar."

"Charlie Edwards," Reesa patted his knee. "welcome to the team. Jamie! I've recruited another one!" she called to her friend.

Jamie rang the small bell on her counter in enthusiasm.

"You girls are going to drive poor Theodore crazy if you're not careful." Billy Lou grinned.

"He's already crazy," Jamie replied. "Crazy *in love*."

Reesa gushed at that, and Billy Lou patted her knee. "That he is."

"That girl of yours, Reesa, has a mind for cars," Charlie complimented. "I was impressed with her yesterday. She knows her way around an engine."

"She's sort of constantly shadowed Theo every second she gets," Reesa explained. "He's impressively tolerant."

"He loves it," Billy Lou assured her. "And it's good for her too. It's good for a woman to know her way around a vehicle. That way if she's ever stranded with a flat tire or something, she knows what she needs to do."

"I was about her age when I fixed up my first car," Charlie reflected. "You remember that ol' '46 Ford two door sedan I had, Billy Lou?"

"How could anyone forget that awful lookin' car?"

"Awful?" Charlie feigned offense. "I thought I'd fixed it up real pretty."

"Charlie, you and your daddy pulled that ol' car out of a chicken house, and it forever carried feathers and smelled like dirty, wet hens."

Charlie laughed, the deep rumble making Billy Lou crack a small smile. Reesa's eyes bounced between them. "Alright, I'll admit it wasn't my best work. But it was a start, and it only cost me $40 at the time."

"Can't say no to a bargain like that." Reesa grinned.

"Not at all. I was tellin' your girl that story yesterday. I apologize in advance, because she said she's already been looking for an older model vehicle for her and Theodore to fix up. Now I think she's searching with gusto."

Reesa shrugged. "If that's what she decides to do, I have no doubt that's what will happen. She and I have a thing for fixing up old things."

"Good to get a little grease on the hands every once in a while," Charlie concurred.

"Speaking of," Reesa giggled. "I think Teddy was a bit surprised when he rolled up to the house to pick Clare up and she had grease smudges on her clothes."

"That boy is so smitten with her, she could be wearing a potato sack and he'd think she was the prettiest thing he's ever seen." Billy Lou smiled as she sipped her coffee.

Charlie watched the interaction between

the two women a moment longer before excusing himself. "Well, I best get after it. It was a pleasure bumping into you two ladies this morning. Billy Lou, always good to see you."

"You've seen me twice," Billy Lou stated, her right brow arching high into her hairline.

"And both times a sheer pleasure," he restated with a smug smile. "Reesa." He tapped his forehead as if he were tipping a hat. "And you, pretty lady," he called to Jamie as she stood behind the counter restocking croissants. "You've plum made my day with this coffee. I think I might just have to make this my morning stop from here on out."

"That's what I like to hear! You come back anytime." As soon as the door closed behind him, Jamie whistled. "BILLY LOU!" She held a hand to her heart. "He is drippin' with charm. How are you able to sit there and not faint?" Jamie fanned her face.

"Honey, I am old. I am tired. And I am not going to fall in love with Charlie Edwards. I have a wonderful life in the house my wonderful husband and I built together. There's no room in my life for someone else. Jerry will always be it for me."

The younger women were quiet a moment and then Jamie leaned her elbows on the counter thoughtfully. "Think he likes younger women?"

Reesa burst into laughter as Billy Lou's eyes widened in shock.

"Only slightly kidding." Jamie giggled. "He's dreamy. I bet he was a real looker back in the day too."

"He was. He was also trouble," Billy Lou warned.

"Oooooh, I like trouble." Jamie wriggled her eyebrows.

"I don't think you can win this one, Billy Lou." Reesa nodded towards her enthusiastic friend. "Jamie's in love."

"Yep. I think I am. I'm officially the new president of the Charlie Edwards fan club."

"Oh, dear Lord," Billy Lou mumbled. "Why on Earth would you be a fan of his?"

"Because," Jamie pointed at Billy Lou. "I see the way he gets you all flustered. There's something about him that gets under your skin."

"I don't care for him. Never really have. Never will."

"What did he do to cause you to dislike him so much?" Reesa asked.

"He was just a straight up troublemaker. He was always lurking beneath the bleachers during ball games. He'd flirt with all the girls, never committing to one, breaking all the hearts after he moved from one to the other. It's no surprise to me that he never married. He was wild, rambunctious, arrogant, and worldly. There was no taming Charlie Edwards."

"Everything you just said makes me all gushy inside," Jamie squealed. "Because what if he's a totally different man now? What if all that was just a front and he was secretly this amazing guy you never even really knew?"

"Then I'd say, it's been fifty years. What does it matter now?" Billy Lou stood. "You girls are always fun. And I love that your young hearts believe in love and romance still. I've had mine, and I'm content with how my life is now. I also know I need to go dig up some carrots over at Theo's. So, if you need me, that's where I'll be. Reesa, you just send Clare on over when she's ready."

"I will."

"Take care, Jamie. See you on Monday."

"Yes ma'am, Billy Lou." The women watched her leave.

"You think they'll ever hit it off?" Jamie asked.

"I don't know, but the tension between the two of them was rather thick, wasn't it?"

"Yes!" Jamie fanned herself again. "There's history there for sure."

"We have to respect Billy Lou's wishes, though, and she doesn't seem like she's wanting a new romance. Theo said she still falls into small pits of depression over losing her husband. Honestly, I can't even fathom the depth of that loss, so I could see how it would be easy to experience those kinds of days." Reesa sighed. "But I just love her so much, I want her to have someone special and someone to take care of her. She takes care of everybody else in this town. I think she deserves a second chance at romance so someone can do the same for her."

"I agree with you." Jamie tapped a finger to her lips in thought. "But how do we encourage such a thing when Billy Lou knows when we're up to something?"

Reesa beamed. "We get Theo to like him. Billy Lou values Theo's feelings on people more than most. If he likes Charlie and also says good things about him, then maybe Billy Lou's mind, and heart, will open up a bit."

"Possibly. But even T.J. might have a hard time thinking of her with someone other than his grandpa. Mr. Jerry was the nicest and loveliest man in town."

"Yeah, the stories they tell make him seem like he was an incredible man. But she wouldn't be replacing him."

"But she might feel that way." Jamie's usually bright attitude fell a bit as sympathy for Billy Lou settled over them both. "I do hope one day Billy Lou could let someone close enough to take care of her though. She deserves to be treated like a queen."

"I agree." Reesa picked up her purse and stood. "I guess we'll just have to see what happens or if Charlie is even worth this much enthusiasm. Time will tell."

Reesa shouldered her bag. "Billy Lou was headed to Theo's place to work in the garden. Clare will be doing the same, and Theo will be done at the garage early this afternoon."

"Girl, say no more." Jamie smiled. "Go and enjoy your Saturday."

"And hey, who knows? Maybe Theo will invite Charlie over for a burger or something this afternoon and I'll gauge the situation more."

"Backyard cookout is the perfect laid-back setting to get to know someone." Jamie pointed out the ingenious idea. "But you know Billy Lou would be upset if she's covered in dirt and sweat and company rolled up."

"True... though that might make things more interesting."

"You're bad," Jamie laughed. "Just remember, woman in love, that not everyone is after the happily ever after that you've found. Billy Lou is a woman who knows her own mind and heart."

Reesa nodded soberly. "Oh, I know. I would never do anything to hurt her, so if I feel like it's a hard no, then I'll stop pursuing the idea. It's just, right now, I'm not sure if it is. Hold me accountable." She pointed to her friend and Jamie nodded.

"Will do. Now, get. Have fun today. I'll see you tomorrow."

Waving, Reesa slipped out the entrance, her steps heading in the direction of her small car.

ˆ

"Sweetie, you have more talent in that pinky of yours than I ever did at your age," Charlie complimented Clare as she wiped her hands on a grease towel and handed it back to him.

She looked at Theo. "I have to go now. I told Billy Lou I'd help her with the carrot situation."

Theo nodded.

She then turned her smile on Charlie. "This is super cool, Mr. Charlie. Thanks for letting me take a look at it again."

"Anytime. It'll take me a couple years to get it runnin' again, so best to look at it now, so when I'm finished you will see how far it comes. Though I'm thinking of swapping this 4 cylinder out with a V-8," he mumbled as he disappeared beneath the hood again to tinker. He could hear the other two talking.

"We should help him with it, Theo."

"I fix cars and trucks and motorcycles and…"

"Yeah, yeah, yeah, you don't want to. I get it," Clare whispered in disappointment, which made

Charlie's lips twitch as he pretended to be occupied a bit longer beneath the hood to give them privacy.

"Think Billy Lou would mind if I helped him?" Clare asked.

"Why would she mind?" Theo asked.

Clare's eyes widened at his lack of notice. "Because she obviously doesn't like him. She gets all irritated if we even mention his name or presence."

Theo shushed her but her comment struck Charlie as odd. What did Billy Lou have against him? Yeah, he left town years ago and never really came around, but that had nothing to do with her. They weren't close in high school or even that good of friends, so why would she dislike him?

"We'll have to talk about it with your mom," Theo explained to the girl.

"Okay. Thanks, Theo. This would be a neat project to be a part of, even if it is just me watching him do it. Alright, I'm going to go dig up carrots. Anything else I need to do in the garden?"

Theo shook his head as Charlie stood back up and straightened his stiff back. "You're good. I saw your mom drive by a while ago, so she may be at the diner still. Catch a ride if you can. If she's not—"

"I'll have Teddy take me. I saw him park over at

the coffee shop a bit ago."

"And you didn't beg me to leave?" Theo's brows lifted. "That's new."

Clare's cheeks blushed as she playfully shoved him away from her. "I was checking out Mr. Charlie's truck."

"Wow, already bitten by the bug," Charlie chuckled. "Honey, I've put these ol' vehicles before everything else in my life for my *entire* life. Don't do the same."

Clare hugged Theo in farewell. "I'll see you around, Mr. Charlie. Thanks again."

Charlie waved as she bounced across the street in long strides and headed toward the cute red-head's coffee shop. "Oh, to be young again." Charlie smiled. "I don't think I'd actually want to, even though I do envy her high energy levels." Charlie shut the hood of the pickup. "Alright, I think it'll make it home. I plan to start disassembling it over the next few days. I appreciate you lookin' it over with me."

"Anytime. If you get to a point you need another pair of hands on it, let me know." Theo nodded to Charlie's cramped hands, a problem that had only recently been giving him fits now and again. He knew it was probably arthritis, but he was bound and determined to ignore it as long as possible. It was just another sign that he was growing older and a hiccup in his day to day he didn't want to have to make time to deal with. The fact that Theo noticed his fumbling with tools earlier because of it irritated him further. But the young man was being kind and didn't state the facts to make Charlie feel incapable, and he appreciated that.

"Will do. You go enjoy your Saturday afternoon with all those pretty women." Winking, Charlie gave him a pat on the shoulder.

Theo turned to walk back into his office and paused. He faced Charlie. "You know, we plan to toss a few burgers on the grill later. About five. Why don't you stop by?"

"Oh." Charlie, surprised by his offer, considered. "Well, you know, that would be fun. Sure."

"I'll let Reesa know." Theo nodded. "At the first road on the right headed out of town towards Hot Springs. A cabin."

"Got it." Charlie tapped his head in salute and watched as the younger man walked back into his office to gather his belongings. He'd hurry to move the truck out of the bay so Theo could lock up. He appreciated the young man's professional opinion, but he also appreciated his willingness and kindness to offer him a relaxed evening with some company. Charlie hadn't really made new friendships in town yet. And most of his contacts from the early days had either left Piney or already passed on, as was becoming more common the older he got. That was the way of things in life. But he welcomed the invitation nonetheless and looked forward to it. He hopped into the pickup and turned the engine over a couple of times before it sputtered to life. Theo now stood outside the bay and gave him a nod as he pulled out onto the road and headed towards home.

His ride home was anything but smooth. The tires needed to be replaced and it was a wonder they hadn't completely blown out the minute he started rolling. The engine died seven times, but thankfully kept cranking back up. Theodore had given him his cell phone number for any roadside emergencies Charlie might encounter, for which he was grateful. But he was determined not to interfere with the young man's afternoon until the cookout. He deserved a break from his work and time with his family.

Charlie reached his daddy's place and pulled into the worn, dirt lane in front of the sagging front porch of the old, white, framed house. Few good memories washed over him each time he looked at the place. He remembered his momma hanging clothes on the line, her pretty work dress and apron and radiant smile. She was the most beautiful woman he could ever remember. Her death had rocked their world growing up. His daddy never coped with losing her. None of them did, really. He and his two brothers practically raised themselves once she was gone. Depression hit his daddy like a semi-truck, and then the alcohol contributed to an even more volatile situation. Charlie and his brothers learned quickly to do things themselves, or just to do without, because none of them were going to ask their daddy to do more than just keeping the roof over their heads. He couldn't have handled any more than that in the state he was in most days. He'd never grown physical with the boys, but Charlie remembered the yelling and screaming, the constant tiptoeing around the house when his old man was passed out on the couch so they wouldn't wake him and suffer the drunken wrath that would immediately follow. That's why Charlie spent most of his time out in the garage tinkering with cars. He couldn't be inside. He couldn't be around the darkness, the sadness, the memories that lingered inside the house of his bright, lovely mother and his soured father, so he escaped. And instead of into a bottle like his father, he immersed himself in grease, parts, and tools.

As soon as he graduated high school, he left Piney. As the youngest of the boys, his last two years of school were just he and his daddy at home, and Charlie made every effort to make that time as minimal as possible. Sure, he got into some trouble as a kid by being a little too much of a free bird, but overall, he felt like he kept his daddy's secret hidden. His family life was private. And even being back in Piney, very few ever really knew his daddy. Lots of "Oh, what a nice man. Kept to himself" or "You know, he didn't do much in town, but he worked hard." His daddy was always good at hiding his pain and his alcoholism. When Charlie received word that his daddy had passed, he came to see what had become of the family place. His brothers both already having passed on as well meant that Charlie inherited what was left of their old life. And by the state of the house, it wasn't much. He wasn't surprised to see the condition of the place. He felt a slight pang of remorse that his daddy lived in such a place, but most of that was the man's own fault and choice. The house was almost uninhabitable. Charlie had been cleaning it out since he arrived and had yet to sleep inside its walls due to the bug infestations, the smell, the mold, and the critters. He had his work cut out for him to get the house in liveable condition before he sold the place. That was his plan, anyway. He didn't anticipate living in Piney. Too many soured memories haunted the steps he took walking around the property. It was a beautiful spot, but it just wasn't for him.

So, he'd clean everything up, repair, fix, maybe remodel a bit, and then sell. And then, it'd be on to the next adventure.

Chapter Three

"*Theodore Whitley,*" Billy Lou placed the second five-gallon bucket on his deck and wiped a dirty garden glove across her forehead. "Next year, you need to pay more attention to how many seeds you drop into the ground. Poor Clare is still out there pulling up carrots and this is our second bucket!"

Reesa rubbed an affectionate hand on his arm and squeezed his hand as he listened to the scolding and relaxed in his patio chair.

"I have no idea if I'm going to have enough jars to put all these away, so now I'm going to have to make a trip to Hot Springs at some point."

"I can get them for you, Billy Lou," Reesa offered.

She waved away the attempt at calming her down. "When you start digging potatoes, Clare and I are retired. Clare!" She yelled for the girl and waved her over. "Let's get us a glass of iced tea and cool down a minute. We've earned it."

The teen didn't have to be told twice. Her original enthusiasm had been replaced with quiet resignation in completing her task. She hopped to her feet and ran from the garden to the deck with Trooper, Theo's black lab, hot on her heels.

Billy Lou walked back out of the house holding two glasses, handing one to Clare and then taking a long sip of her own. "And who on Earth drives a white pickup like that?" Billy Lou pointed over her shoulder as a late model Ford bounced up the dirt road to the cabin.

"Oh, that's Charlie Edwards," Theo stated. "I invited him to supper."

"You did what?" Billy Lou barked.

"I invited him," Theo restated. "So be nice."

"Why would I not be nice?" Billy Lou looked offended. "I'm always nice. I just wish you had told me sooner so that I would have prepared."

"Prepared what? I'm doing the cooking." Theo's confusion had Reesa chuckling.

"She would have primped." Reesa winked at Billy Lou and though she denied the charge, Billy Lou could feel her cheeks flushing at the insinuation.

"Not at all. I just don't like being caught unaware."

"I show up at your house all the time uninvited." Clare looked concerned that she may have been offending Billy Lou all this time and Billy Lou felt her heart squeeze.

"Oh no, honey, I love when you come see me. I just meant... well, Charlie and I go way back, and he wasn't and isn't a person I would like to be around."

"Why not?" Reesa asked.

"He's just a rough one, that's all."

"How so?" Clare asked. "He seems nice to me."

"Oh, he always was, but there's more to him than meets the eye."

"Grandma—" Theo stood to his feet and Billy Lou sized him up.

"Don't you Grandma me. I said what I said, and he is what he is."

"That was a long time ago. I'd sure hate for someone to hold my past against me."

"Me too," Reesa chimed in. Billy Lou knew both of them struggled with that very insecurity and it made her crumble.

"Okay, you two. I'm not talking about either of you. I would never hold your pasts against you, and I'm not doing that to Charlie. It's just from what I can tell, he hasn't changed all that much. So I'm just going to say this to all of you: be cautious around Charlie Edwards. His daddy was a hardworking man and all three of his boys deserted him. You don't desert family."

Reesa's face fell slightly and Billy Lou, once again, felt the fool. She'd forgotten about Reesa's estrangement from her parents and knew the woman had been attempting to rebuild connections with them over in Hot Springs. The struggle was a difficult one on both sides. And she knew Reesa carried years of guilt for not reaching out sooner.

Theo tenderly squeezed Reesa's hand.

"I didn't mean..." Billy Lou covered her face with a dirty glove. "Honey, you know I didn't mean you."

"I know, Billy Lou." Reesa offered a polite smile, but Billy Lou could see the subtle hurt she'd inflicted.

"See, he gets me so worked up I don't even know what I'm saying." Billy Lou shimmied her shoulders. "Alright, you invited him. Go greet him, then." She waved for Theo to get up and meet Charlie at the steps while she collected herself. Clare followed Theo, excited to see her new acquaintance.

"Reesa, sweetie, I did not mean to hurt you, honey."

"I know, Billy Lou." Reesa accepted Billy Lou's extended hand.

"I'm just battling my own demons when it comes to Charlie Edwards, and I seem to be lashing out those feelings on those around me."

"Why does he get under your skin so bad? What happened between you two?"

"Absolutely nothing," Billy Lou replied honestly. "I just look at him and think, 'Why is he still here?' Jerry had to die, a man with a loving family, a legacy. And Charlie Edwards, the great deserter of Piney is allowed to come in and have a second chance at a life when he turned his back on his own family and this community so long ago. It just doesn't seem fair. And it irritates me. That's just my grief talkin', I know it is, and I'm trying to tamper that down and not be such a pill about it. But that man was no good back in the day, and he doesn't seem to have changed much."

"You've had two conversations with him, Billy Lou," Reesa reminded her. "Don't you think you're projecting a bit? So far, he's been kind and friendly. He may have been a bad guy fifty years ago, but he seems to have somewhat changed considering that he's been nothing but friendly since he's been back. I think we all need to just keep an open mind and remind ourselves that people *can* change."

"You bring up a good point."

"And, if I'm overstepping here, I apologize, but sometimes we need hard truths," Reesa continued. "And if you get upset with me, I'm sorry for making you so and I hope you'll forgive me but...

your losing Jerry isn't Charlie's fault. And your anger over losing your husband seems to be aimed at him right now." She grimaced as if she were afraid to bring up the truth and Billy Lou's shoulders sagged. Her words hit home. It was true that Billy Lou was still ticked off the good Lord took Jerry from this world sooner than she wanted, and seeing Charlie Edwards swoop into town happy and healthy after being such a terror all those years ago irritated her. Her loss magnified when she looked at him and she couldn't help but project her hurt and bitterness over her loss onto him. She would need to work on that. She knew it. But grief was a funny thing; she never knew when it would sneak up on her, but for some reason it tended to when Charlie was near.

"I appreciate you, Reesa, honey. I need to do better. And I will. You keep holdin' me accountable, okay? Even when I don't want to hear it." She hugged Reesa in a tight embrace before releasing her.

"My goodness, those are some carrots." Charlie eyed the full buckets and then nodded in greeting towards Reesa and Billy Lou. "You've been busy."

Billy Lou dusted some dirt off the knees of her capris with her garden gloves. "Clare and I are dedicated to the task."

"It would seem so. What do you even do with so many carrots?"

"I'll can most of them. Maybe flash freeze a few,"

Billy Lou replied. "Though I'll be cannin' for days." She narrowed her eyes at Theo.

"My momma used to can all kinds of stuff too." A soft smile teased the corners of his lips before his eyes turned sad and he changed the subject. "Nice place you have here, Theo."

"Thanks." Theo offered Charlie a beer and the man shook his head. "No thanks. You have some of that tea, though? That sure looks good." He nodded towards Clare's half empty glass.

"I'll go get you one." Clare hopped off the porch railing and darted into the house.

"Have a seat." Reesa pointed to a free patio chair. "There's some bug spray if you need it. The mosquitos aren't too bad right now, but in about an hour, it'll be survival of the fittest."

Charlie chuckled. "Never really understood why God created mosquitos."

"They had a different purpose before the fall of man, I'm sure," Billy Lou replied. "As did most things."

"I bet they were like bees," Clare replied thoughtfully, handing Charlie his glass. "Meaning, maybe he intended for them to pollinate things, but then they turned into little blood sucking vampires."

Reesa chuckled as Theo smirked. "Vampires, huh?" Theo asked.

"Well, yeah, they suck blood," Clare pointed out. "Too bad they don't die in the sun though, right?" She grinned as Charlie laughed.

"No more talk of vampires. You'll give me, or yourself, nightmares," Billy Lou warned.

"Vampires don't scare me." Clare shrugged. "Lore says they can't come into your house unless invited, so I think we're safe there. Plus, the last time we had an intruder, Mom took care of him." A sly smile spread over her face as she looked at Theo.

"Like a banshee," Theo mumbled, and Reesa swatted his chest on a laugh.

"I think I'm missing something," Charlie whispered to Billy Lou.

"Oh, Reesa attacked Theo when he came in the middle of the night to capture an intruder. She mistook him for the intruder and fired on all cylinders... with pepper spray. Turns out the intruder was just a pesky raccoon, but poor Theo took the lashing of a lifetime."

"Good for her protectin' her nest." Charlie nodded.

Billy Lou's eyes sparked. "Yes, but Theo was in rough shape too."

"Pepper spray is the worst," Charlie admitted. "I bet that lingered for a few days."

"It did." Clare giggled. "Theo used to have this *awful* bush man beard and he had to shave it off.

Which, honestly, we are all thankful for."

"I'm still sitting here, Clare." Theo's dry response sent her into a fit of giggles as Reesa patted his leg.

"Don't even act like you aren't grateful," Clare replied. "After that, Mom couldn't keep her eyes off of you."

His brow lifted slightly, and he turned to face Reesa. She just nodded in agreement. "It's true."

Billy Lou hooted in laughter as Reesa unashamedly leaned over and kissed Theo's sour expression. "These two have brought a lot of fun to Theo's life the last few months."

"I can see that." Charlie took a sip of his tea.

Theo stood.

"Uh oh, he's uncomfortable now," Clare continued teasing. "He's going to disappear under the guise that he's prepping the burgers."

Theo turned to her in surprise, and he sighed. "How do you know me so well? It's eerie." He winked at Reesa on his way into the house to assure her he wasn't bothered, and she settled comfortably back into her chair.

"So, Charlie," Reesa began. "How long are you in Piney for? Or did you move here permanently?"

"Well, I'm not sure yet. I don't plan to stay, but I've got some work cut out for me."

"Like what?" Clare asked.

"Well, my daddy didn't really take care of the family house and it needs some work."

"Maybe if he'd had some help, it wouldn't be so bad," Billy Lou murmured before taking a sip of her drink, her sharp eyes holding Charlie's a brief second longer than polite. She wanted him to know her feelings on his abandoning his father over the years.

"What all do you plan to do to the place?" Clare asked, blissfully unaware of Billy Lou's quiet disapproval.

"Well, right now I'm just cleaning it out. Then I'll move into the mapping out a plan stage. But the cleaning is going to take me a while yet."

"Need help?" Reesa asked.

"Oh, now, I wouldn't ask for that kind of help. It's in terrible shape. I don't even like steppin' foot in there, so I don't plan on askin' anyone else to." He smiled at Reesa and Clare. "But I thank you for the offer."

"It didn't look that bad the other day when I was there with Theo." Clare replied.

"The outside is just a bit faded and droopy, that's true. But the inside is another matter," Charlie replied. "Years of... neglect," he finished.

"Clare and I have done some renovation projects in the past," Reesa continued. "If you want a pair of fresh eyes one day, just let me know."

"I'll keep that in mind." Charlie toasted his tea glass towards her before taking a sip.

"You have more than enough to keep you busy, Reesa," Billy Lou interrupted. "Besides, it's Charlie's responsibility."

"But—" Clare started and then choked back any further words when Billy Lou looked at her. "Yes ma'am," she muttered before rising to her feet. "I'm going to go help Theo." She hurried off and Reesa eyed Billy Lou in suspicion.

"I think I'll carry these buckets to the car." Billy Lou stood, and Charlie pointed to one of the buckets.

"I'll get those for ya, Billy." He stood and she waved him away.

"I don't need *your* help." Her sharp retort had him pausing long enough she was able to swoop the buckets away and around the house.

⌃

A car door shut, the sound bringing Charlie out of the run-down house carrying a loaded trash bag full of old newspapers. He tossed them into a burn pile he'd started the day before and looked up to find Reesa standing at the base of his porch. "You weren't kidding." She smiled in greeting.

He slipped his leather gloves off his hands and tucked them in his back pocket as he wiped one sleeve over his sweat-stricken face. "Yep. It's in a sad state."

"Has good bones though." She patted the porch railing with affection. "I imagine you've been floating down memory lane as you go, too. A house like this is bound to carry a few."

"I try to avoid those, actually."

Her eyes turned sympathetic before she squared her shoulders. "I came to apologize."

"What on earth for?" Confused, Charlie waved her away from the house and toward the folded down truck bed of his pickup where he had a cooler full of waters. He offered her one and she accepted in kind.

"For yesterday evening. Billy Lou—"

"Is not for you to apologize for," he finished for her. "She's her own person and her own mind."

"Well, I'm sorry she was rude to you," Reesa continued. "To be honest, it's not like her to be like that. At all."

"I don't take it personally." He shrugged his shoulders. "I have a feeling there's more to her disliking me than I'm aware of, but at the same time, I think she just gets mad when she looks at me because I'm not Jerry."

Reesa's look of acknowledgment to his words told him he'd hit the nail on the head.

"She's still grieving him. And look, I know my reputation here in Piney. No one likes me."

"Why would you say that?" Reesa looked shocked.

"Because of my daddy." He nodded towards the dilapidated house. "People think I up and abandoned him in his old age. What kind of person could possibly do that?" He took a sip of his own water as his eyes looked over the faded house.

"It's not really anyone else's business, though," Reesa argued.

"This is Piney. It's everyone's business. Or have you not been here long enough to know that?"

She smirked. "I guess you're right, but I've also lived other places and lived long enough to know that there's usually more to someone's story than what meets the eye."

His eyes narrowed on her a moment and she pointed to an old pen off the side of the house. "Pigs?" she asked.

He appreciated the subject change and walked alongside her, the overgrown pecan trees shading their path. "Pigs, goats, cows, chickens. Whatever we had at the time. There was always somethin' in these old pens. My brother, Tommy, was in charge of most of the animals."

"And where does he live now?" Reesa asked.

"Oh, he's passed on now. My other brother, Randall, as well. It's just me now days."

"I'm sorry." Her voice rang with a touch of empathy but her eyes were clear as she studied him.

"Thank you. I'd like to say we were close, but we weren't. All of us just couldn't wait to leave this place. Once we all did, we never really looked back or *at* each other."

"That's tough."

"Sad thing is, it wasn't, really."

"I've sort of done the same thing. My parents and I are, well, were estranged for years. Only recently have I really reconnected with them. And even then, it's really just my dad. My mother... well, she still hasn't come around yet."

"Good on you for trying. Sometimes it's hard to let go of the past and look at the possibilities of a future."

"It isn't easy, but we've been keeping at it." Reesa smiled warmly.

"Keep up the fight, then. Don't let yourself end up like ol' me. Old, never married, alone, and tired." He chuckled to make the depressing tone of the conversation a little lighter.

"Well, I hate to break it to you, Charlie Edwards, but you've met Reesa and Clare Tate. Unfortunately for you, whether you like it or not, we will never leave you alone." She grinned. "It's part of our charm."

He chuckled. "You know, I can see that."

Her eyes danced a moment before she gasped. "What is that?" She darted across the yard to a stack of wooden crates filled with glass jars.

"Those are my momma's old cannin' jars. We used to plant a garden, over there." He motioned to an open space east of the house. "Every year we'd make us up a decent-sized patch and my momma would can the excess."

"That's amazing." Reesa lifted one of the old, empty jars. "Man, the old jars have some heft to them, don't they? Clare would love to see these."

"You can take as many as you like." Charlie waved his hand over at them. "I'm just going to be donating them all."

"I can have them?" Reesa asked.

"Sure thing."

"Billy Lou was just talking about how she needed to buy more jars for the carrot canning project. Would she be able to use these?"

"Sure, after she cleans them up a bit. She'd have to buy new lids, but I imagine they'd still work just fine."

"Great! I'll take them off your hands. I may even keep a few for me to do some sort of craft with..." Her words trailed off as he watched her mind whirl with ideas. "As long as you're not sentimentally attached to them," she finished.

"I'm not. I've got the one thing I love the most of my momma and that's the color of her eyes. I don't need anything else other than that to remind me of her. Besides, just walkin' around this place, I'm reminded of her every step I take."

"Good memories?" Reesa asked.

"Of her, yes. Always good memories," Charlie assured her. "She was the most beautiful woman you could imagine. There's some pictures of her somewhere in there, I just haven't found them yet. Not sure if I will. Knowing my daddy, he probably burnt them years ago."

"How sad. I hope that's not the case."

"Me too. Time will tell."

"Mind if I take a look at the house?" Reesa pointed to the open door.

"If you aren't scared of bugs." Charlie chuckled as he motioned for her to follow him up the creaking steps. "Watch your step here when you walk in. Got a broken floorboard that needs fixed."

Reesa stepped into the gloomy room and her hand immediately covered her nose and mouth. "Oh my."

"Yep. The smell is terrible."

"What is that from?"

"Best I can guess is the three dead coons I found in the corner of the room when I first got here."

"Dead animals?" Her eyes widened.

"Yep." And there's an odd smell coming from the fireplace too, so I'm not sure if there's something up the chimney or not yet. Haven't gotten there."

"But... how... why... how are you living here?" she asked, her eyes bouncing from one atrocity to the next.

"I'm not."

"Where are you stayin'?"

"In my truck mostly, though the pastor lets me come to the church and use the shower before he locks up for the evenings."

"Charlie." Reesa fisted her hands on her hips. "You cannot be serious. This is not okay."

"Oh, it's not too bad. Once I get the house cleaned out, I can get to cleaning up things and repairing. Might be able to stay in it then."

"But that could be weeks or months." She swatted a cobweb out of the way as she walked down the hall. "How long ago did your dad pass away?"

"About two months ago."

"Two months!" Reesa turned stunned eyes his direction. "There is no way this house got *this* bad in just two months. This is caused by years of neglect, not months."

Charlie stuffed his hands in his front pockets. "And now you see why I never really came home."

"Bless your heart." Reesa shook her head in dismay as she continued through the house. He heard her gasp and then an excited shout from down the hall. "Love this fireplace in the master bedroom!"

He smirked. She was a gem, and he appreciated her enthusiasm despite the circumstances and conditions of the place.

She came back down the hall towards him. "Okay, so you are not doing this alone." He started to open his mouth and she held up her finger. "No, you can't say anything yet. This is too much work and you need it done fast so you're not sleeping in your truck. Which, by the way, ends tonight. You'll stay at Theo's. I'm calling him." She pulled out her cell phone and he objected. She held up her hand and spoke into the receiver. "Theodore Whitley, get your butt to Charlie's. Now." She hung up. "Has he seen this? Does he know you're sleeping in your truck?"

"Honey, I've done it before. I appreciate you wanting to help, but I'm alright. I assure you."

Less than five minutes later, Billy Lou's sporty SUV pulled up in a huff of sand and gravel. She hopped out with the speed of a cheetah and only once she saw Reesa emerge from the house did her shoulders relax. She marched up the stone path towards the house.

"Billy Lou?" Reesa looked confused. "What are you doing here?"

Billy Lou held a hand to her heart, her eyes narrowing at Charlie as he emerged beside Reesa. "Theo said you called in a panic and that you were here at Charlie's. I was closer so I came immediately. What is going on? What happened?"

"Nothing happened," Reesa assured her. "Is Theo coming?"

"Yes, he is. He was on his way. Let me give him a buzz to let him know you are okay. You are okay, aren't you?" Her eyes pinned Charlie like a flea beneath a fingernail.

"Yes, I'm completely fine," Reesa stated again and rubbed a reassuring hand on Charlie's back. "Actually, it's good that you came anyway." Reesa motioned for Billy Lou to follow her. "Charlie has some jars he's getting rid of. I thought maybe we could use them for canning." She pointed to the crates and Billy Lou turned to look at him.

"All of these?"

"Yes ma'am. Yours if you want them."

"Well, they're in horrendous shape, but I think we could make them shine again." Billy Lou lifted her key fob and her trunk automatically opened. "Let's load these up and I'll take them home with me."

Charlie began lifting a crate.

"Reesa and I can do it. No need for your help."

"Billy, I'm—"

"It's Billy *Lou*. Stop calling me Billy. I haven't gone by Billy since high school."

"Alright, I'm sorry." Charlie held his hands up as if surrendering to whatever death match she had up her sleeve. "I can carry these to your car."

"We can do it."

"I'm sure you can, but I'm not gonna let you." Charlie stepped by her and lifted two crates and made quick work of navigating the lumpy yard towards her car.

Theo pulled up and he hurried towards Reesa. Charlie didn't hear their conversation, but Reesa motioned to his truck and his house multiple times. Billy Lou lingered near them, her eyes watching him move the crates himself as she listened. Theo walked towards him and Charlie turned after sliding the crates into Billy Lou's car. "I told her not to worry about me."

Theo smirked. "You don't know, Reesa."

"I think I'm beginning to." Charlie wiped his hands on a handkerchief and then stuffed it into his back pocket.

"I've got an extra room and bathroom," Theo stated. "It's yours as long as you need it."

"I don't want to intrude on you, and I certainly don't want to—"

"Charlie Edwards, you old fool!" Billy Lou called across the yard as she exited his house with Reesa.

He hadn't seen them walk inside, but Billy Lou cleared the yard faster than the woman half her age. "You will stay at Theo's. There is no sense in you stayin' here. Don't be an idiot. Now, I'm going to take the jars to my house, and Reesa is going to come over and help me clean them up. We'll see both of you at supper." She walked to her car and hopped inside. They watched as she buckled her seat belt and motioned for them to move out of her way. They immediately did her bidding and she drove away.

"Is she always that bossy?" Charlie asked.

"Yes," Reesa and Theo stated at the same time.

"Best pack your bags, Charlie, because she will make sure you followed her orders." Reesa pointed at Theo.

Feeling awkward at such an offer, Charlie looked to the younger man.

To lighten the mood, Theo motioned to his truck at a ball of black fur and slobber marks on his window. "Hope you don't mind dogs."

Chapter Four

"*Pilaf. That's a fun* word." Clare sat across from Billy Lou and sliced strawberries for their dessert as Billy Lou stirred the simmering pot in front of her.

"It's just a fancy way of saying rice boiled in broth."

"Interesting. That's seriously the only difference from regular rice?"

"Pretty much." Billy Lou smiled. "But you don't make rice in regular water anyhow, ya hear. Broth, no matter the kind, adds a richer flavor."

"I feel like I should add this to my Billy Lou notebook." Clare hopped from her seat.

"Notebook?" Billy Lou watched her retreating back and looked at Reesa in confusion.

"She keeps notes on everything you teach her so she'll remember when she graduates and moves off," Reesa explained. "Theo was teaching her the viability of seeds. Total snooze fest, but that girl wrote down everything he said. Complete with doodles."

"That is just the sweetest thing. Well, I hope it helps her later on down the road."

"Oh, it will. I'm not a cook, as we all know, so any tips in that arena are all welcome." Reesa switched to Clare's seat and picked up her task of slicing strawberries.

Clare returned and began flipping through a black notebook to find a blank page. "Okay, from the top. How do you make Rice—" She paused to write the recipe name at the top of her page. "Pilaf?" she finished and then eagerly looked at Billy Lou.

"Oh, sweetie." Billy Lou reached across the counter and squeezed her hand before leaving her position and wandering over to a cabinet lined with cookbooks. "Let's see... ah, here it is." She withdrew a well-worn book from the shelf and flipped through it and then slid it across to Clare. "Rice Pilaf. The recipe is from my momma. This is a book she put together for me for when I got married."

"Oh wow." Clare tenderly turned the page. "Chocolate Pie! Okay, I'm loving this. Wait, it says to cover it with a Tuesday towel. What's a Tuesday towel?"

Chuckling, Billy Lou walked over to the same cabinet and removed a stack of tea towels. She set them gently on the counter and then pointed to the hand stitched images and words along the bottom. "Each towel has a day of the week embroidered on them. My momma believed Tuesday was a twice blessed day, so when she baked, she considered it an extra blessing on her dessert if it was covered in the Tuesday towel." Billy Lou grinned. "I think it was more to just keep us kids out of it."

"That's amazing." Clare brushed a finger over the cross-stitched pattern. "And she made these?"

"Actually, I made this set when I was in my early twenties. I have several sets. Over the years towels get stained, burned, or lost and so I'd make new ones when I could."

"You cross-stitch?" Reesa asked. "How did I not know this?" She looked at an equally surprised Clare.

"I don't do it much anymore," Billy Lou admitted. "Just one of those things I haven't made time for in a while."

"Well, you should." Clare held up a floral stitched towel to her mother. "These are beautiful, Billy Lou."

"Thank you, sweetie."

"I like these kinds of towels." Reesa fingered the material. "There's a couple at the cabin. Every time I use one, I feel like I'm in some old western movie."

"Western?" Clare giggled. "Why a western?"

"You know, because they would wrap their picnic goodies in these or their bread and leave it on the counter. Oooh, or Mary Ingalls. Yes, very Mary thing to do," Reesa explained.

"Don't you mean, Laura Ingalls?" Clare asked.

"No, I mean Mary. She was the oldest and probably helped their mom prepare the baskets for after church lunch."

Clare just shook her head at her mother's rambling thoughts and looked back at Billy Lou.

"My momma would wrap her bread up in one as well. She swore it helped keep it moist. Though she had to make bread every single day; we ate it up while it was still warm, so I don't know why she even bothered wrapping it, really." Billy Lou walked back over to the stove top and lifted the lid on her pot of rice. "I think that will about do it on that." She turned off the flame beneath it. "Now, let me check on the chicken breasts in the oven." She walked across the room and opened the top door of her double ovens. "Looking good as well."

"Smells amazing," Reesa called. "Should I fix glasses?"

"Not yet. I don't even see Theo and Charlie yet."

"They pulled up a while ago." Clare flipped a page in the cookbook. "I think they're in the garage looking at the Corvette."

Billy Lou's brow lifted. "Oh?"

"Car junkies." Clare shrugged her shoulders. "I take a peek under its cover every time I walk by it too."

"Is that so?" Billy Lou laughed.

"Don't even get me started on that fabulous car." Reesa flexed her fingers. "That time I drove it... we connected. I think it will forever be imprinted on my mind and fingers." She gripped an imaginary steering wheel. "A hauntingly beautiful muscle memory that teases me in my dreams."

Billy Lou swatted her with one of the extra towels and Reesa laughed. "You two are silly. Anytime you want to take that car for a spin, you're more than welcome."

"Don't tell her that." Clare shook her head in dismay at Billy Lou's blunder.

Reesa nudged her daughter as the door leading to the garage opened, and Theo and Charlie walked inside. "About time." Reesa stood to her feet and walked over to Theo. She slid her arms around him and looked up in adoration, Billy Lou masking her joy at how tenderly her grandson, the gruff Theodore, gently brushed his thumb over Reesa's cheek before lightly kissing her.

Charlie stood awkwardly to the side, but Clare, blessed with her mother's outgoing spirit, patted the stool next to her. "Have a seat, Mr. Charlie. I'm just over here looking at Billy Lou's recipe books. Top secret information, in case you're interested." Billy Lou laughed at the girl's antics as Charlie seemed to relax and took a seat next to Clare. "Look at this one. I don't know why it's called that, but it sure sounds interesting. Could be gross or oddly delicious."

Charlie chuckled and looked up at Billy Lou. "She's on Watergate Salad." He turned his attention to Clare. "And it's oddly delicious."

"Can I write this one down too, Billy Lou?" Clare asked, her pen already hovering in her notebook.

"Honey, you take that with you and you write down whatever you want to."

"Really?" Clare's eyes rounded.

"Yes. It'll give you some good recipes to experiment with."

"Thanks!" Clare excitedly thumbed over another page.

Billy Lou's eyes sharpened on Charlie. "You get settled over at Theo's?"

"I did." Charlie nodded. "Nice place, nice guy you have there, Billy Lou."

"I think so." She beamed over at her grandson who was now listening to Clare go on and on about the recipe book.

"I'm going to do my best to get out of his hair within a week. Don't want to overstay my welcome."

"You better find help or some superpowers then, Charlie Edwards, because that house needs a lot of tending to."

He sighed and glanced at his weathered hands, and Billy Lou noticed him rubbing and massaging around his knuckles. "Yeah... just got to keep at it. It'll come along."

She walked away mid conversation and he sat quietly as she returned a few seconds later carrying a small bottle. She slid it to him.

"What's this?"

"Cream. For your hands."

"What's wrong with my hands?" Charlie asked.

"They're hurting you. And they're dry. They're hurting you, aren't they?" His cheeks deepened in color and he didn't answer. "Trust me. It works. I use it on mine every night before bed because my joints are so sore by the end of the day." Billy Lou nodded for him to put it in his pocket on his shirt. "Use it, Charlie. We're old now. We need hand creams." Her lips twitched a bit, and he returned the amused gaze as he slipped it into his shirt pocket.

"I refuse to accept the fact we are old," Charlie admitted.

"Oh, I accepted it a long time ago," Billy Lou replied. "And I actually quite love it. No one can tell us what to do now. That's our job. The power is glorious." She winked at Theo as he nodded in agreement on his way to the refrigerator.

"She sometimes lets it go to her head," Theo murmured.

"No such thing, Theodore." Billy Lou blushed when the two women agreed. "Well, now. I guess I just won't feed the lot of you if you're going to gang up on me. You hooligans." Everyone smiled as she walked back over to the oven to check the chicken. "And it's a real shame because supper is ready."

^

"Reesa, you start in the back bedroom. I'll start in the other and we'll work our way towards the front." Billy Lou looked at Charlie as he stood next to her.

"I told you to go home, Billy." She fisted her hands on her hips and he added, "Lou," remembering that she now insisted on such. She had her white hair tied back with a silk scarf like Rosy the Riveter, the bright floral pattern carrying roses as pink as her lipstick and pulling her hair off of her face. She had a beautiful face. She'd always had that to her credit, and he liked the look of it even now. Life had not worn Billy Lou Waldrup down, and he was glad. His own face on the other hand seemed to drastically age day by day. He didn't even recognize the man in the mirror anymore, and he certainly didn't feel as old as he looked. But he'd take it in stride like he did most things.

"What are you staring at?" she asked, her hand self-consciously reaching up to touch her hair.

He smirked and lightly brushed a fingertip over her head band. "Just thinkin' about how pretty you are."

That stunned her. Her lips moved as if she wanted to say something, but no sound came out. "Well—"

Charlie grinned. "I'll get on." He walked towards the empty trailer Theo had borrowed from a friend and began loading the mounds of trash and debris he planned to dispose of as Billy Lou disappeared in the house. He'd made good work of the pile when a loud scream came from inside the house. He dropped the load in his hands and sprinted as best he could up the stairs and towards the back bedroom. By the time he reached it, Billy Lou and Reesa were in a fit of giggles. "What happened?" he panted.

Billy Lou stood next to him in the doorway and pointed to a trapped Reesa who was half way between the floor and a hole beneath. She held on to the floorboards with a tight grip. "Oh yeah..." Charlie's eyes danced.

And Billy Lou swatted his chest. "Well, help her."

"Right." Charlie jumped to it, grabbing Reesa's hands and lifting her like she weighed no more than a bag of potatoes. His eyes looked down the hole. "I forgot all about this."

"Root cellar?" Billy Lou asked.

"No." Charlie reached in his back pocket and withdrew a flashlight, shining it down the dark hole. "I'll be—" He sat and began sliding himself down into the hole.

"What on earth are you doing?" Billy Lou hurried forward and she and Reesa peered over the opening.

"Tommy and I dug this out when we were kids." He circled the small space. "A safe room, I guess you could call it. We'd hide from our daddy down here. It started out as a tiny hole that barely fit the two of us, but we worked on it for years. By the time we were in high school it was our secret hideout."

They heard him gasp.

"Charlie, you okay?" Reesa called down.

He lifted a dusty leather photo album up through the hole and she took it. She flipped open the front cover. "Your mom."

"I guess Tommy found them and saved them from Daddy's wrath before he could destroy every memory of her. There's a whole box of her stuff down here." His voice cracked as he tried to mask the swell of emotion in his chest. A foot kicked him in the shoulder and he looked up to find Billy Lou dangling half way in the hole. "What are you doing, Billy?" He reached up and grabbed her petite waist to ease her down to the floor. Her eyes darted around the small enclosure, and she smiled at the old high school photos of Charlie and his brothers. She even came across a group photo that had Jerry standing alongside Charlie, their arms thrown over each other's shoulders.

"When was that?" she asked curiously, not even aware they'd been friends.

"Oh, that was mechanics class. I'd fixed Jerry's pickup as my semester project and somehow— mostly by the grace of God— I got it to work. We celebrated my passing and his new set of wheels that day over at the soda shop. He bought me a float. That was the first float I'd ever had." Charlie tugged on the photo and the rusty thumb tack fell to the ground. He handed her the photo. "We hung out a lot that year at the school garage. Got to know one another. We still ran in different circles, but he was a nice guy. I've never forgotten that float. Every time I have one now, I always think of that day. That was the day Jerry told me he was going to marry you."

Her eyes bounced back up to his. "He did?"

"Yep. Y'all weren't even dating yet," he chuckled. "But you walked in with Ivy Grands and Emma

Jane Butler, all of you wearin' your little cheer uniforms. Jerry looked at me and said, "That's her. The woman of my dreams. Whaddaya think, Charlie? Think I can marry her?'" He laughed at Billy Lou's shock. "I told him he'd better hurry because there wasn't a boy in school who wasn't thinkin' the exact same thing. He walked right up to you and asked you to the drive-in that night."

"I remember that," she whispered.

"And I believe, he was a man of his word. He married you." He smiled at her and tapped the picture. "You keep that. That was the day Jerry asked you out. Special."

"Well, thank you for telling me that story." Billy Lou swiped a tear from her eye. "Seems so long ago."

"Doesn't it? Yet, it also seems like it was yesterday. This house has been making me remember a lot of things. I'm glad to find a room that has good memories instead of bad."

She tenderly brushed a hand down his arm. "Well, maybe we'll get it all fixed up and you can make new, better memories here."

"I don't intend on keeping the place." Charlie reached for an old shoebox and began thumbing through the contents. He held up a half dollar. "Now that would buy a nice sized float for sure. Think that pretty red head would hook us up?"

Billy Lou nodded. "I bet she would. I bet she'd do

just about anything you ask her, because she wants to marry *you*."

Charlie, baffled, looked at Billy Lou in complete shock. "Why on earth would she want to marry me? I'm old."

"Oh, but you're handsome and intriguing, the usual reasons women get all in a tizzy." Billy Lou waved her hand as she spoke and he reached for it, giving it a gentle squeeze. "Well, I guess my future awaits, then. Come on, Billy. Let's go get us a float." He lifted her up and she gripped the floor to pull herself out of the hole. A smiling Reesa stood in the doorway holding a pile of old linens with vintage floral patterns. Charlie hefted himself up and turned off his flashlight.

"Can I have these?" Reesa asked, holding up the stack.

"Honey, you can have whatever you want, but right now, we're all going to the coffee shop to get us a float. Come on. I'm going to treat you girls."

Reesa's brows rose but she didn't argue.

"He found a fifty-cent piece and now thinks he's rich," Billy Lou added.

"Hey, back in the day I would have been." He winked at her before passing Reesa to go outside. He heard the young woman whisper something to Billy Lou but he couldn't hear Billy's response.

He opened the passenger door of his truck. "You

ladies want a ride?"

Reesa beamed and set her linens on the front porch rocking chair. "Shot gun!"

"There's only a front seat," Billy Lou retorted but didn't argue as she slid into the middle and Reesa climbed in next to her. Charlie shut the door and rounded the hood. He couldn't remember the last time he took a woman for a drink of any kind. Not that he was reading too much into this, but he liked opening his door and hearing the chatter between the two women, and the sweet smell of Billy Lou's perfume as she sat beside him. For the first time since seeing him, she didn't pull away at his touch when his shoulder bumped hers as they drove along the bumpy driveway. She still held the picture of him and Jerry and began naming the other people in the photo for Reesa.

"You have to show this to Jamie." Reesa's eyes bounced to Charlie. "Though I must apologize in advance, Charlie, because this is only going to make my friend like you even more."

He laughed. "That boy was a handful," he said, talking about himself as he glanced briefly at the picture.

"You're just making yourself more appealing." Reesa grinned as they pulled into a parking spot outside of Java Jamie's. She hurried inside to chat with her friend as Charlie helped Billy Lou out of his truck and shut the door.

They walked inside and Jamie gushed. "Woo! Look at you, Mr. Charlie!" She fanned her face with the photo. "I knew you were a looker now, but back in the day..." She fanned herself again. "I told Billy Lou the other day that I'd found some new eye candy." She winked at him. "What can I get ya?"

"I'm treating these girls to whatever they want."

"Ooooooh! Handsome *and* a gentleman." Jamie winked at Billy Lou. "Reesa said something about coke floats. I have the makings if that's what you want."

"For me, yes." He looked at Billy Lou and she nodded.

"And me," Reesa agreed.

"Alright, I'll bring them to you." She waved them away from the counter and he slipped his half dollar in her tip jar.

"Spending it all in one place." Billy Lou shook her head in mock dismay and his chuckle made her smile. His heart warmed at the sight, and he liked that they seemed to find some common footing now; that she wasn't angry or sad when looking at him, but that maybe, she'd come to see him as a potential friend.

Jamie bounced over and delivered three floats and sat on one of the free chairs. "Now, tell me, what's got you three all dusty and dirty."

"My house," Charlie admitted. "These two beautiful

ladies are helping me clean it out."

"Oh, right!" Jamie snapped her fingers. "I remember you telling me about helping." She looked at Reesa. "Oh, and I have something for you, Mr. Charlie." Jamie disappeared into one of her back rooms and emerged with a picture frame. She flipped it around and an old oil painting of his parent's house stared back at him. Only, instead of the neglected house it was now, it was an image of what it had looked like years ago before his momma had passed.

"Where did you get this?"

"I painted it." Jamie smiled.

"But... how did you know what it used to look like?" He pointed to the sheets hanging on the line west of the house, and the luscious garden to the east. It was exactly how he remembered home from his boyhood.

"Oh," Jamie sat again and handed him an old photograph. "I was in the courthouse one day, back when I was thinkin' I might like to answer phones for a living and work in the clerk's office. Yeah, it wasn't for me," she giggled. "But this older man came in with a whole box of old stuff and lots of photos. He felt like they might have historical significance to the town, which some of them did. There were pictures of downtown from the early 1900s and such. But then I saw this photo, and I loved that house. There was just something about it. I asked if I could have the picture and they said yes. I painted this a couple of years ago. It wasn't until Reesa started telling me about your house that I realized it sounded like this one."

"Wait—" Reesa looked at her friend in stunned silence. "You paint? How have we not talked about this?"

Jamie blushed. "I don't really tell people or show people my work. This was just too *"WHAT?"* not to."

"All these hidden talents just coming to the surface. Billy Lou cross stitches, you paint. Charlie, anything you secretly know how to do?" Reesa looked at him and he shook his head, his eyes glued to the canvas in front of him. Billy Lou gently rubbed a soothing circle in the middle of his back.

"This is... this is like a time capsule. Thank you, Jamie." He reached over and gripped the young girl's hand. "And beautifully, artfully, done."

"Well, like I said," Jamie expertly shoved off the compliment and stood. "it's yours. It's been sitting in my studio for two years. Will be good for it to see some sun."

"Studio?" Reesa looked even more bewildered and Jamie laughed.

"Well, thank you, sweetheart." Charlie looked at the aged photo and just shook his head. "I just can't believe it. This is what I remember it looking like while Momma was still with us. Those were her favorite tablecloths on the line. I can tell by the trim pattern. Amazing." His voice trailed off and he covered his lips with his hand to hold back emotions he hadn't realized crept up on him.

Jamie smiled at her friends and rushed to the counter to help a new customer. Charlie sat quietly studying the painting and the photo. He cleared his throat and set the painting gently beside his chair and slipped the photo in his shirt pocket. "That will be a nice picture to hang over the mantle when I get the house finished."

"And now we have a visual to help us along the way. End goals, so to speak." Reesa nodded towards the photo.

"Still an us, hm?" Charlie, amused, bounced his gaze from one woman to the next.

"You betcha, Charlie Edwards." Billy Lou nodded in agreement with Reesa. "Now, let's finish these floats, because now we have to figure out a way to get that floor in that room up to code. And I know just who to call." Billy Lou whipped out her phone.

"Mr. Wright!" Jamie yelled from behind the counter and did an excited little shimmy dance as Reesa laughed and rolled her eyes.

"Oh boy, here we go," Reesa murmured, her eyes apologetic when she looked at Charlie. "I hope you're ready for all of us, Charlie."

Beginning to think he just might be, Charlie smiled. "Ready as I'll ever be, sweetheart."

Chapter Five

Billy Lou, always grateful for an invitation to Theodore's house for a meal, pulled her SUV next to his work pickup in the driveway. She didn't see Reesa's car, but she imagined Clare and Reesa walked through the woods instead of driving. But to her surprise, when she walked inside the house, Theo was alone. "I thought you'd have a full house." Billy Lou placed a pie, covered in a Tuesday towel for Clare's enjoyment, on the counter.

"Reesa and Clare will be here in a bit. Teddy had come by to hang out with Clare, so Reesa was letting them enjoy some more time together before heading this way."

"Oh, sweet Teddy Graham. Has he asked Clare out

yet?"

"Not that I know of. They're still 'just friends.'"
Theo air-quoted the term and Billy Lou grinned.

"I guess that is good. They're awfully young to be
thinking of romance anyhow."

"Says the woman who married at seventeen." Theo
walked over to his refrigerator and removed a
bowl of marinating meat.

"It was different back then."

"Not really." Theo shrugged his shoulders. "You
just got lucky."

"That's true." Billy Lou smiled. "Did Reesa tell you
about the old picture Charlie found of him and
your granddaddy?" Theo nodded. "I didn't even
know they were friends back then."

"You mean there is something the great Billy Lou
Whitley *didn't* know? I find that hard to believe."
Theo smirked as his hands dove into the meat
mixture and he began shaping a long loaf.

"What in the world are you making?" Billy Lou
asked.

"Meatloaf."

"That is not how you make meatloaf, Theodore."

"It's how I make it."

"Well, that's not right. You have to put it in a dish
first."

"Why?"

Billy Lou sputtered in disbelief. "That's how you get it to shape properly."

His hands continued to work on the meat, and he disregarded her comment. He set one mound aside and began shaping another.

"Where is Charlie? Isn't he staying here?"

"He is. But he's not here."

"Why not?" Billy Lou asked.

"Because he can come and go as he pleases, Grandma." Theo shook his head at her nosiness. "I'm not his keeper. Besides, he has his hands full with the house and the old truck."

"Oh, so he's tinkering, that's why he's not here."

"I don't know. I'm just assuming." Theo walked to the sink and washed his hands, then grabbed a ball of mozzarella cheese from the refrigerator. He began slicing pieces and placing them on top of one of the meatloaves.

Billy Lou watched as he then moved the second half on top and covered the cheese, molding the shape into one single loaf. "You stuffed it with cheese?"

"A Reesa tip. She likes it this way."

"I've never even heard of such."

"Maybe you should try it. New things aren't always

so bad."

"I didn't say they were." Billy Lou felt her hackles rise. "I've just never seen someone prepare meatloaf in such a way, Theodore."

His lips tipped at the corners, and he continued his preparations.

She glanced at her watch. "It's almost five-thirty. Where is everybody?"

"I told them supper at 7, so maybe they're keeping busy until then. Oh, by the way, Reesa's dad is coming into town tomorrow to visit. I think she plans on a quiet supper between just the three of them."

"Her momma still not paying her any mind?"

"Not yet." Theo walked to a basket on his counter and grabbed three fistfuls of fresh green beans from his garden collection and tossed them in a colander. He then rinsed them in the sink. "Roger has grown more and more comfortable with each trip. He seems to enjoy Clare and has connected with her."

"Well, she's an amazing girl. Who wouldn't?" Billy Lou eased onto the stool across from Theo and set her purse on the one next to her. "Poor Reesa, though. Virginia Tate better get her act together or I'm going to drive all the way to Hot Springs and have a few words with her."

"It's not your place," Theo warned.

"I'll make it my place. She is doing nothing but purposely causing heartbreak for sweet Reesa. No mother has the right to do that, especially when Reesa is just wanting Clare to get to know them. I'm glad Roger is coming. I'll try to bake up some cookies to drop off to her tomorrow so she'll have them on hand."

"For him? Or for Reesa's stress eating at the idea of him coming?"

"Both. Bless her heart." A car door shut, and Billy Lou hopped to her feet. "That must be the girls." She swept towards the front door and opened it wide, a beaming smile on her face. It fled as soon as she saw a surprised Charlie standing there, covered in dirt, cobwebs, and grease. His eyes lit in amazement at the sight of her warm welcome. "Oh." Billy Lou motioned him inside. "I thought you were my girls."

"Sorry to disappoint." He hefted two grocery sacks to the kitchen and set them on the counter. "Theo," he greeted, Theodore giving a slight nod at his return. "Got us a new tub of ice cream." He began stowing his groceries, Billy Lou's watchful eyes soaking in the two men navigating one another in the kitchen as if they'd been roommates for years. She saw him place a pack of cream sodas in the refrigerator, the old timey glass bottles clanking together as he did so. He handed Theo a small loaf of bakery bread.

"Thanks for picking this up."

"Not a problem." Charlie folded up the two grocery bags and placed them in a pile by the back door.

"Well, you get her taken apart?" Theo asked.

"Mostly. I still have the main frame to do, but the exterior and interior pieces are now scattered about the shed. Was a nice break today to just work on that and not the house."

"And?"

"Not rusted as badly as I thought." Charlie seemed pleased and Billy Lou listened intently as the two men chattered back and forth about Charlie's old pickup project.

Theodore seemed comfortable with Charlie, which wasn't her grandson's norm with new people, or people in general. She even caught him smiling a few times as Charlie spoke about small adjustments he wanted to make or do to the vehicle. Odd, she thought, that it didn't bother her as much as she thought it would to see Theo bonding with another man besides Jerry. Theo and her late husband had always had a special bond, and sometimes even Billy Lou felt like an intruder on their time together. She felt similarly now. Why was Theodore so chummy with Charlie? What was it about the man that had her grandson so willing to open up his home to him? It couldn't just be at the request of Reesa. Even though Theodore valued his girlfriend's opinions, he was still Theodore, and the idea of having a long-term house guest would have never been on the table as even a consideration. But yet, here she was, witnessing a budding friendship between Charlie Edwards and Theodore. She wasn't sure how she felt about it. Not yet, anyway. This entire conversation should have been with Jerry, not Charlie. A heavy, slow, and familiar pain began creeping through her chest and she felt the sudden pang of tears threaten to spill. She reached for Theodore's gardening bucket. "I'm going to check the garden." She hurried out the back door, both men glancing curiously at her retreating back.

She made it behind the tall corn stalks before the first sob escaped her lips. She bit it back and attempted to control the sudden wave of devastation that took hold of her. She missed Jerry. She wanted Jerry. She loved Jerry. And yet, she was mad at him for not being present anymore. It wasn't his fault, she knew that, but the pain was still raw. Even after a couple of years, she missed him on a daily basis. His company. That was one of the biggest things she missed. Her house felt empty without him. She loved when Theodore or the girls came by her place because the house didn't feel so vacant then. She didn't feel so alone. At night, she struggled. She'd even picked up her cross stitching again since the other day, hoping that losing herself into a project for Clare would help distract her from the fact that she was sitting in her living room alone, quiet, with only the television for company. It wasn't how she envisioned living. She loved her home. She loved her memories. She loved Piney. But sometimes, that love carried a weight that she wasn't sure she wanted anymore. To live with loss was not fully living. Embracing that it would always be a part of who she was also wasn't enticing. But she had. And she did. And she was still living and breathing and loving. There was just a hole, a Jerry-sized hole, that painted a light hue of grief to the rest of life's moments. She was grateful for the years they had together, but loneliness was now her companion. She soaked up the days with her friends and family because the nights were long and quiet and lonely.

She heard a rustle coming from the tree line and saw Reesa, Clare, and Trooper walking from the small cabin over to Theo's. Trooper spotted her first and excitedly ran over, dancing around her feet until she gave him the loving scratch behind the ears he expected.

"Hey, Billy Lou." Clare hopped up next to her and hugged her around the shoulders in a tight squeeze.

"Hey, sweetie. How was your day at school?"

"Long." Clare gave an exaggerated teenage sigh. "But I didn't have to work at the garage today, so I was able to hang out with Teddy for a bit and that was fun."

"I'm glad to hear it. You girls hungry? Theodore's got an interesting meatloaf he's preparing in there."

"Is Mr. Charlie here?" Clare asked excitedly.

"He is." Billy Lou motioned over her shoulder to the house.

"Cool. I was hoping to introduce Gramps to him tomorrow. That's what Roger said I could call him." Clare beamed. "Gramps. I picked it. He said it was perfect." She hurried passed Billy Lou into the house and Billy Lou caught Reesa's eye.

"I'm glad your father seems to be making an effort with Clare. Seems like they're getting along."

"Oh, like two peas in a pod." Reesa smiled. "Dad's been great. He really has just embraced us, but it's hard for him still with Mom being... not as open yet."

"I do believe she will eventually come around. How could she not? Especially if he and Clare grow closer. She'll want to be a part of that as well, and by extension, want to know you more in the process."

"I'm not sure if it will work out that way, but I'm going to stick with it. Charlie gave me some good advice on that the other day."

"Charlie?"

"Yeah, you know, since he didn't really keep up with his brothers or dad and what not. I mean, we both sort of faced circumstances that weren't normal, and unfortunately it affected our relationships with our families, but he said he regrets losing touch with his brothers now. I don't want to have that same regret with my parents.

Mom will just have to deal."

Billy Lou smiled and gave Reesa an encouraging hug. "You'll win her over, sweetie. You have more charm and determination in that pinky of yours than most people have in their entire lives."

"Some people would call that charm and determination stubbornness." Theo's voice interrupted them, and Reesa's eyes lit up as he descended the stairs towards them. "I need a bell pepper." He pointed to his garden.

"You were just escaping Clare, be honest." Reesa chuckled as he didn't confirm nor deny and went straight to his pepper plants. "She was excited to see Charlie and talk to him about his truck project."

"I gathered that. She's talkin' like a regular grease monkey in there."

"Your own fault," Reesa pointed out. "Oh, wise one of mechanics." He smirked as he walked back towards the house. "I like those jeans on you, by the way!" she called after him, and he turned an embarrassed look her way as she wriggled her eyebrows.

Billy Lou hooted in laughter as he quickly slipped back into his house. "Oh, honey, you are so good for him." She lovingly patted Reesa's arm. "Come on, let's go see if he's almost done with supper."

As their steps coordinated into a leisurely pace,

she felt Reesa studying her profile and she hoped the young woman couldn't tell she'd been crying. "Somethin' on your mind, honey?"

"Yes—" Reesa paused a moment. "But I don't want to overstep."

"Out with it," Billy Lou encouraged.

"Okay," Reesa paused, bending to pet Trooper as he companionably walked beside them. "Have you ever thought about dating anyone?"

Billy Lou rolled her eyes. "Is this you and Jamie trying to play matchmaker again?"

"Not really. I was just curious. I mean, I cannot imagine what you've been through Billy Lou. Honestly, I can't. But I also... well, I love you. And I think you deserve someone to love you and take care of you all the time. Not just when we pop in for some of your awesome cooking or to visit, but someone to be with you all the time. And just— well, I don't know, love you again."

Billy Lou pulled Reesa into a tight hug. "Those are sweet words, my dear. And I love that you believe me worthy of them and worthy of someone's affections. But I have what I need for now. I love my life the way it is, and I love that you and Clare have come into my life and into Theodore's. I'm content."

"But—" Reesa paused. "Okay, I'll drop it for now." They walked a few more steps. "But can you at least admit he's handsome?"

"Who?" Billy Lou asked.

"Charlie."

Billy Lou laughed. "Charlie Edwards has always been handsome. His problem is that he's always known it."

"He doesn't seem arrogant to me," Reesa mused.

"Perhaps its softened some in his old age."

"But he is handsome," Reesa continued, nudging Billy Lou's shoulder with a sly smile.

"He is. I'll give him that."

"And nice," Reesa prodded.

"So far."

"And—"

"I thought you were dropping this topic?" Billy Lou asked in amusement.

Reesa's cheeks flushed. "Right. Done. No more from me." She pretended to zip her lips and toss the key away.

"Good." Billy Lou looked at her and placed her hands firmly on her lips. "Now tell me how you came up with a cheese-stuffed meatloaf."

Grinning, Reesa led the way up the patio stairs towards the back door. "Everything is better with cheese, Billy Lou. Everything."

"Hmm." Billy Lou chuckled. "I'll try to remember

that."

They opened the door to an excited Clare holding up Billy Lou's pie. "Mom, look! A Tuesday towel!"

^

"T.J. you have to come. It's our fifteen-year reunion. Everyone will expect you to be there." Jamie bounced behind the counter of her coffee bar and whipped together three coffees. One for Theo, the other two for his mechanics at the garage.

"Not my thing, Jamie."

"I know, but you could bring Reesa with you. She'd be a hit. Plus, we'd all get to hang out in a non-casual setting, be dressed up and eat good food. Listen to some classics from our heydays. Talk about people. In hushed tones, of course." She giggled.

"Didn't you just see these people at the ten-year reunion? Why are they doing fifteen years? Don't places just do like ten, twenty, etc.?"

She waved away his comment. "We have a vigorous and connected class president and team, I guess. Besides, you didn't go to the ten-year reunion. Remember, you stood me up."

He looked offended. "I did not stand you up. I wasn't in town."

"I know, I'm teasing." She giggled in her usual

bubbly way that made him smirk. "Well, maybe Reesa would be my date then."

"You would take my girlfriend as your date to our high school reunion?"

"Why not? We're friends. And I want to have fun. Reesa is fun. And she'd appreciate my dress." Jamie beamed as the door to her shop opened up and Charlie Edwards walked inside. "Better yet, I have a another idea. Mornin', Mr. Charlie. I've got a question for you."

"Morning, beautiful," Charlie greeted, and Jamie's excited eyes danced towards Theo for a moment.

"What can I get you besides a hot date two weeks from now?" Jamie asked curiously.

Charlie's brows rose up into his hairline. "A date?"

"Yep. You and me, handsome. A date."

His cheeks flamed at being put on the spot and for being asked out by a woman drastically younger than him. "Well, I, um—"

"See, he's speechless." Jamie waved her hands up in the air in victory. "Think on it, Mr. Charlie. I've got a high school reunion coming up and T.J. refuses to come, and I need a date."

"Honey, you don't want to take an old fogey as your date. You're too pretty for the likes of me."

"You're exactly who I plan to take." Jamie winked at him. "Two weeks." She held up two fingers and then her smile blossomed even further. "I think this is my most exciting morning in weeks. Mornin', Billy Lou!"

Charlie turned to see Billy Lou enter the coffee shop dressed in a classy outfit of white capris and a royal blue blouse with bejeweled sandals over perfectly pedicured feet. She screamed class and sophistication. "Hi honey. Theodore. Charlie." She greeted them all and then looked to Jamie. "My usual, sweetheart, in a to-go cup. I'm headed to Hot Springs this morning."

"Will do." Jamie's hands busied themselves behind the counter. "You always have a knack for showing up at the perfect time, Billy Lou. I was just trying to convince T.J. to come to our high school reunion in a couple of weeks, and I was just trying to win Mr. Charlie here over with my charm to be my date. I need some Billy Lou help with both of them."

"Reunion? Date?" She looked at Charlie in confusion and he felt the blush climb up his neck and to his cheeks once again at even being considered for such a role.

"Yep." Jamie laughed as she bagged up a couple of chocolate hazelnut croissants to go with Theo's order, free of charge. "They're both playing hard to get."

"Theodore, you will go. You didn't go to the last one and it's important."

"Grandma, I love you, but I'm old enough not to be bossed around."

Billy Lou's brow lifted in challenge as she pulled out her cell phone and pressed a number. She hit the speakerphone button and Reesa's voice flooded the line. "Mornin' doll. Guess what? Theodore's high school reunion is coming up in—" She looked at Jamie and she held up two fingers. "In two weeks. He's a bit nervous about goin' and could really use your support."

"Of course! It will be fun. Oooooh, I'll get a new dress. Maybe Jamie will help me shop for one. Wait, Jamie will be there too, then, because they went to school together. Perfect! I'm in. I'll talk to him and encourage him to go."

"Thanks, honey." Billy Lou's voice dripped with sweetness. "You really are the best thing to ever happen to him. Love you. See you soon." She hung up. "There. Problem solved. Theodore will be attending, Jamie."

Theo stood solemnly to the side and just shook his head. "Y'all are impossible," he muttered, but his eyes told them he was only slightly annoyed at the intrusion.

"That was just downright brutal." Charlie chuckled and then swallowed when both women's eyes turned on him.

"Yep, his turn, Billy Lou. I need a hot date, and he's holding out on me." Jamie placed a hand over her heart as if wounded.

Instead of helping Jamie by convincing him, Billy Lou picked up on his awkwardness and looked to her young friend. "Well, honey, Charlie can't go with you. Though he's flattered, he just can't. He's already committed to the children's hospital charity fundraiser dinner with me over in Hot Springs. Sounds like it might be the same night."

Jamie and Theo's eyes widened in surprise at her statement, and Charlie shifted his stunned attention on her. "Maybe you could ask Jason to be your escort?"

"Mr. Wright?" Jamie looked baffled. "He'll be there already, and I guarantee he wouldn't consider me as his date. I'm not... well, I'm not his type." Jamie looked disappointed at that fact, but she smiled anyway. "But at least I'll have Reesa and T.J. there. We'll be a team."

"Exactly." Billy Lou smiled as she handed Jamie cash for her coffee. "I'll see you three later." She buzzed out the door without a second glance his direction and Charlie stood in stunned silence.

"Sounds like you need a suit," Theo murmured. Jamie squealed in excitement and had both men laughing.

"I guess you're right." He took his coffee from Jamie, and she winked at him. "You two stay out of trouble." He pointed at her specifically and she held up her hands in innocence as he walked out the door. Billy Lou was just opening her car door as he passed by. "What's this about a charity dinner?"

She looked at him. "I go every year. It's formal. You'll need a suit. I hate bow ties, so please find a decent necktie. I'll be wearing a plum colored dress."

"Is this you asking me to go with you? Or you just going to boss me?" Charlie asked curiously.

"I was under the impression I was saving you from a high school reunion." Billy Lou's brow quirked as she studied him. "Unless you were wanting to be the old geezer amongst children."

He frowned. "When and where is this dinner?"

"Second Saturday of next month. Hot Springs. It starts at six. We'll need to leave around four. You can come to my house and we'll take my car."

"Anything else?" he asked.

Billy Lou's eyes held his for a moment and she softly smiled. "You're welcome."

He harrumphed and he heard her chuckle as she slid into her driver's seat and buckled her seat belt. "Don't look so dumbfounded, Charlie."

"I'm just trying to figure out how I got outmaneuvred by two women in a matter of seconds."

"We're good."

"Clearly."

"Take care." Billy Lou shut her door and backed out of the parking space, leaving him standing there still in complete surprise.

"Get used to it," Theo's voice called as he began walking down the sidewalk towards his garage. "The women around here are masterminds."

"And what are your thoughts?" Charlie asked.

"About what?"

"About me escorting your Grandmamma to a charity fundraiser."

Theo stopped walking and faced him. "Don't kill each other and I'll be fine with it."

Charlie smirked. "I'll do my best." He tapped the top of his head as if he wore a hat and then walked to his pickup. He sat a moment, staring at the coffee shop's exterior in front of him and then chuckled to himself. Who would have thought he'd be taking Billy Lou Waldrup on a date?

Chapter Six

Jason Wright, the best carpenter Billy Lou had ever worked with, surveyed Charlie's house and the hole in the back bedroom floor. His flashlight grazed over the interior of the dark space, and he looked up at Billy Lou. "Doesn't seem to have affected the integrity of the house structure. It's just a giant hole and the floor doesn't have support. Could add a few piers and beams under here. Add new flooring support and it should be just fine."

"Good. Charlie!" She yelled down the hallway and then sighed. "I think he went back outside. Hold on, Jason." She hurried off as Charlie was making his way back into the house. "Come on." She grabbed his arm as she led him down the hall. "Jason says it's not that bad and shouldn't be too difficult to fix."

"Well, that's good."

When they entered the room, Jason was climbing up out of the secret room beneath the bedroom floor. "Nice work down there, Mr. Edwards."

Charlie rubbed a hand over his chin. "Not bad for a couple of kids."

Jason smiled. "I would have loved that as a boy too. I've got a couple of ideas for you if you want to hear me out."

"Yes sir." Charlie waved the young man back outside so they could discuss it outside of the dingy old house.

Billy Lou watched the two of them as she scrubbed the fireplace stones with a steel brush and a strong concoction of baking soda, vinegar, and dish soap to take the years of grime off the pretty white stones. Charlie hadn't asked her to come help, she'd just felt the need to do so after spending an entire day the day before in Hot Springs shopping and doing frivolous errands. She needed some physical labor that made her feel useful. Granted, she'd found a pretty necklace to go with her dress for the charity dinner in a couple weeks, so the trip wasn't completely wasted. And she'd grabbed groceries, of course, a few odds and ends for Reesa and Clare, and purchased Theodore some new shirts because they were on sale. Taking care of her ducklings, she'd felt rather at ease browsing the racks yesterday. But now she was determined to make the fireplace and mantle shine in the old Edwards house. An odd smell still permeated the interior of the fireplace, but Charlie assured her he'd cleaned it out. Apparently, he'd found all sorts of deceased critters and abandoned bird nests in the process. She had to admit, Charlie worked hard. He was never idle, never one to shrug off his tasks, which was surprising since that was her original opinion of him. She still didn't know the full story behind his leaving Piney the way he did, but the more she worked on the sad house, she continued to put things together. The broken, empty liquor bottles were one sign that things weren't what they seemed, and she wondered how long his daddy had suffered from his addiction. Had anyone noticed? She would admit that Johnny Edwards always seemed cleaned up when he ventured into town, but his house told a different story. She never once actually checked on the man, even knowing his family had abandoned him. She felt guiltier and guiltier about that the more she looked around and cleaned. Not much she could do about it now, though, except help Charlie clean up the mess left behind and hope that the house came together for him. She liked having projects and she loved working with houses, so it was a win-win for both of them. It also gave her a purpose. She enjoyed helping people. And she liked to be busy herself.

She heard a crash from outside and hurried out the door. Jason had left and Charlie was working in his shed amongst truck pieces and parts. She heard a growl of dissatisfaction and his mumbling about annoying axles. "You alright in here?" Billy Lou stepped into the shed and Charlie looked up from the heavy tire gripped in his hands. His face was red, but she realized it wasn't from embarrassment, but from strain. His hands looked cramped as the tire sat squarely on top of his foot. She hurried towards him and helped roll the tire off his foot, and helped his hands loosen their grip. She rubbed his knuckles and massaged his hands in hers, working out the tightness and pain she knew he must have been feeling. He hissed a few times from the pain of uncurling and unfurling his fingers. "It's alright, Billy. I'm fine."

"No, you're not. Now stop and let me work. We aren't thirty anymore, Charlie. We have arthritis, aches, pains, and even more stubbornness than we did as kids. It's only part of growing old. Own up to it and let me help you. It always helps when I rub my hands like this. My knuckles get so tight some days, it's awful." She felt him watching her as she continued to massage his hands until she felt them begin to relax. "I think you need to be done in here for today," she warned him. "or I'm going to have to come in here every five minutes." She attempted to sound cross, but in reality, she felt sympathy for him. It wasn't easy for a man like Charlie, a man who used his hands for work and labor, and even for joy as he worked on his cars to have such an issue. And she knew it had to annoy him just as it annoyed her when her hands cramped up.

"I think they're better now." His low voice was quiet in the dusty shed, and she realized she now just held his hands in hers and was studying them. The wide palms, the roughened fingers, and mere strength of them surprised her. She wasn't sure why, but it did. She released them and cleared her throat. "I'll be back in the house. I'm determined to get that fireplace looking as good as new."

"Thanks, Billy." He walked back out into the sunshine with her and added. "Lou."

"Oh, just stop trying. There's no point. You know me as Billy, might as well stick with it."

He chuckled. "Even if it annoys you?"

She sighed and her face relaxed into a sad smile. "Doesn't annoy me. I guess it just makes me aware of how long ago it was that people used to call me that. Makes me feel my age, I guess."

"Well, if it helps, you don't look much different from how you did back then."

"Now that, Charlie Edwards, is a lie."

"Not so." He grinned. "Still the prettiest girl in Piney."

She felt her cheeks deepen in color, but his comment made her heart lift a touch. "Now you're just being foolish."

"Say what you will, Billy Lou Waldrup Whitley, but there's no person in town who would disagree with me." Charlie looked up as Teddy Graham's small pickup truck pulled up in the drive. The young man stepped out, his uncertainty and nervousness evident, but he politely walked towards them.

"Well, hi there, Teddy, honey," Billy Lou greeted him warmly and his demeanour relaxed. "What are you doing here?"

"Mr. Charlie?" He extended his hand towards Charlie and shook. "Clare was telling me about your house project, and I have a work-force class that allows me to leave school early each day to do some work. I have a job part-time in town, but I don't work there every day. I was wondering if you might need a hand on the days I have off?"

Billy Lou appreciated the thorough weighing of Teddy by Charlie as if the young man had something to prove to him, too, regarding Clare. "Clare thinks a lot of you," Charlie stated, and both watched as the boy's ears turned a bright pink.

"Yes sir. I think a lot of her too." He nervously tucked his hands into his front jean pockets. "And she thinks a lot of you, sir."

Billy Lou noticed Charlie straighten just a smidge in pride at that thought, and she liked that he considered Clare's opinion to be valuable. "Well, if you want to get your hands dirty, I think we could use you around here. What say you, Billy?"

"I think so." She beamed in pride as Teddy nodded.

"I'm free now, if you need me today."

"Perfect!" Billy Lou clapped her hands. "I have just the project for you, Teddy. You're young and spry and we need someone to clean out a secret hideout." She looked to Charlie for approval, and he nodded. "Come with me and I'll show ya our little time capsule." She patted the young man on the back on their way across the yard, proud of him for jumping into a new situation with courage.

When she returned outside, Charlie hoisted a large bag full of broken dishes onto the trash trailer.

"He seems like a good kid."

"He is," Billy Lou confirmed. "Good for him to get his hands dirty too. He'll work hard for you. I've got him climbing up and down that hole in there. I was dreading that job."

"You know, I didn't ask you to help me every day either," Charlie pointed out.

"I know. I want to."

"Why?"

"Because you need help."

"But that doesn't mean you have to do it. I have help now, too." He pointed towards the house where Teddy now worked.

"I like having projects."

"And this one is one you'd like to do?"

KATHARINE E. HAMILTON

"Well, sure. I'm here, aren't I?" She fisted her hands on her slim hips.

"I don't want you hurtin' yourself," Charlie added, moving by her to grab another load of trash to toss on the trailer.

"I won't. I know my limitations."

He looked at her doubtful and she huffed. "You're one to talk, Charlie Edwards. Need I remind you of what just happened in the shed?" His back stiffened at her words and he turned in annoyance. "Don't get mad at me. It is what it is, old man. You need my help just as much as that young man in there. If you don't want to admit it yet, that's fine, but I'm helping. No buts about it."

"Because you like projects?"

"Yes."

"And that's it?"

"Isn't that enough?" Billy Lou challenged.

He stepped closer to her and she squared her chin and stared up at him, toe to toe.

"And you ask me to a fancy dinner?"

"I did. To save you from a night out with Theo and his friends."

"Maybe I wanted to go."

She huffed, flustered that he wasn't understanding how much she'd helped him there, or her willingness to help at his house just because she wanted to be a friend. "You didn't. I could tell on your face."

"Oh really?"

"Yes."

"I don't get asked out much these days. Maybe I was thinkin' about it," he continued.

"You were not," Billy Lou ranted. "Because that would make you a complete fool, Charlie Edwards. A fool to think that would even be a good idea."

"But dinner with you in Hot Springs is a better idea?"

"Well, yes. Why wouldn't it be? You'd at least be with someone close to your own age and not looking completely out of your element. And I'm lovely company."

"Is that so?"

"Yes. I assure you, I am," she stubbornly replied.

"Hmm." He grimaced like he didn't believe her, and she swatted his chest. He caught her hand and held it over his heart. Laughing, he leaned down and kissed her cheek. He winked and released her as she stood baffled at what had just happened. "You're starting to like me, Billy, even if you won't admit it."

"I'm not, I assure you."

"You sure do like assuring things." He walked

towards the house, and she was hot on his heels. Her cheek still tingled from where he'd kissed her and she hadn't felt that response since her husband, the thrill of it surprising her. She wondered what Charlie was playing at. She also reminded herself that it was Charlie Edwards in front of her, a man known for leaving when things got tough. A man who never settled down or stayed in one place for too long. And though she'd felt a little excitement in her change of opinion of him, she also knew she wanted to tread carefully. She didn't want to fall for Charlie. She didn't want to fall for anyone. She wanted to be Jerry's wife, whether he was here or not. Her footsteps came to a halt as disloyalty coursed through her at the slightest bit of attraction she'd just felt towards Charlie. Feeling awkward now, Billy Lou retreated back outside. She'd come back tomorrow. She'd covered good ground for the day, and she needed air and space away from Charlie.

He stepped out of his house and eyed her curiously as she hurried towards her car.

"Billy—" His voice trailed off when he saw the tears streaming down her face as she climbed into her car and slammed the door. He took hurried steps in her direction, but she pulled away as swiftly as she could.

^

    Charlie hung up the phone and stood from the patio chair. He reached for his keys. "Got a live one," he commented, Theo glancing up from shucking corn.

"Where at?"

"Ol' Milly Owens' place. Apparently, there's an old pickup caught up in a barbed wire fence that's just been sitting there for decades. She's wanting to replace that fence and needs to move the truck. Said I could have it if I moved it."

"Not a bad deal. Need some help?"

"If you want to ride along, sure. Might be good to have an extra man on deck."

Theo set aside the corn and his scrap bucket. He whistled and Trooper sprinted from the tree line to load up with them. They took Theo's truck in order to tow the old pickup if possible. Charlie had a feeling they'd need to load it on a trailer, but you never knew with these types of calls. He'd gotten several cars over the years from random phone calls about people finding old cars on their property, tucked away or neglected in a garage. Typically, they just want to be rid of them and don't charge him a dime. A few others he'd bought here and there to fix up, but most of his started with just a good old dusty find. He loved restoring them to beauty, making them run. That first drive with the windows down in a newly restored car made his blood pump faster, proud that he'd had a hand in bringing it back to life. He'd made a decent side income from restoring old vehicles. He worked in insurance most of his adult life, and the cars and trucks and even a few tractors kept him sane. When he retired, he was set on only enjoying mechanics, and he had, until he got the call about his daddy passing. Even then, it took him months before he made his way back to Piney. He had a lot to wrap up; he sold his house, packed his bags and came. Now, he not only had a new pickup and probably another new pickup to restore, he had an entire house to do as well. His hands would be full and busy for quite some time. And as much as he originally disliked the thought of spending the rest of his days in Piney, he had a feeling that it was his final place to roost. Full circle, really, and maybe that was fitting.

"Grandma said Teddy is going to start helping out at the house with you." Theo turned down an old road off the main drag to head to the Owens' property. They still had around ten minutes or so if Charlie remembered correctly, the terrain not having changed much this far out of town.

"Yeah, he seems like a good kid. Smitten with Clare, for sure."

Theo smirked. "Yeah, he is."

"And she seems to like him well enough."

"She does, though Reesa isn't a fan of teenage boys lurking around her daughter, even if they are named Teddy Graham," Theo replied.

Charlie laughed. "Well, she's raised a smart one. Clare won't give him attention if he's not worthy of it. She's too smart for that."

"He's got a good head on his shoulders." Theo turned onto another side road, the bumps growing more pronounced.

"And how do you feel about dating a woman with a teenage daughter? What's your role in the conversation?"

"Reesa respects my feelings on it as well. She also knows I will protect Clare. If any boy becomes a problem, I will handle it."

"Good man." Charlie nodded.

"Same goes for my grandmother." Theo's eyes glanced his direction a moment before focusing back on the road in front of him.

Charlie smiled to himself at the man's willingness to lay down the law. "I respect that too, I assure you." He cringed at Billy Lou's favorite phrase rolling off his own lips so easily. "Your grandmother would never have eyes for a man like me, and I respect her too much to even try." He thought about the day before when he'd thought, perhaps, she might have warmed up to him. But he'd overstepped. He'd misread the situation and hurt her somehow. The guilt still ate at him when he thought about her tear-stained face. He'd made the decision right then not to pursue or encourage anything with Billy Lou Whitley. She was helping him and that was it. She was being useful and a good friend. That was it. "She's a gem, though."

KATHARINE E. HAMILTON

"She's been the rock of our family forever," Theo explained. "When Grandpa died, it devastated all of us, but it was like a part of her was gone too. She's recovered well, but that loss is still there."

"It always will be," Charlie replied. "Jerry was a good one. Even back in the day he was genuinely one of the best guys in town. They don't make them like him anymore. No offense. Though I do see a lot of him in you."

"He taught me everything I know, which I guess I should thank you for. I hadn't put it together until Grandma showed me a picture of you and Grandpa together back in the day. He said his love for cars grew because of a kid named Charlie back in school. I didn't realize you two knew each other, but I'm pretty sure that picture tells me you're the Charlie he was talking about."

Charlie pondered that a moment and felt a slight pang of pride at giving the same gift he'd found in restoration. "He ever build street rods?"

"No, Grandpa was just a fan of cars, as is evident by his Corvette that sits in Grandma's garage. She was horrified when he brought that home."

Laughing, Charlie could only imagine a fuming Billy Lou. "I bet she wore him out for that one."

"Oh, she did. He tried to sweet talk her into a ride one afternoon after church, and she told him that car was as red as Satan, and how dare he even ask her that on a Sunday."

Charlie slapped his leg as he burst into a deep belly laugh, Theo doing the same.

"That was the maddest I'd ever seen her. That night at supper, Grandpa stepped lightly around the kitchen."

"I bet he did. Poor Jerry." Charlie shook his head in sympathy for his old friend. "I bet she kept him on his toes. That's good. I'm glad they were happy together."

"You ever settle down?" Theo asked.

"Nope. Never found the right one, I guess. To be honest, I never really looked. I spent most of my time working and traveling. Then when I'd be at home for long stretches, I'd work on cars. Time just flies in life. I'll also admit I was a selfish man for the first forty to fifty years of my life, so there's that too. Hard to factor in someone else when all you think about is yourself."

"And what changed that for you?"

"Life." Charlie shifted in his seat and readjusted his seat belt. "Maturity. Priorities change as you get older, and a giant slice of humble pie on the side tends to help too."

"I've always liked being on my own." Theo slowed as two deer crossed the road in front of them. He patiently waited as the smaller of the two hesitated and stared at them a moment beneath the pine-canopied back road. "And then Reesa showed up."

Charlie chuckled. "Yeah, I hear women can rock a man's world."

"It was irritating at first," Theo admitted. "She was just always there. Even when she wasn't physically present, she had somehow woven her way into my life in other areas that I couldn't ignore her anymore. And then I realized I didn't want to."

"She's a force, I'll give you that."

"And then there was Clare to consider. I never really thought about kids: wanting them or having them." Theo sighed. "And she weaselled her way into my life too. The two of them are a package deal."

"This you thinking about making it a permanent situation?" Charlie asked, curious if this was the young man's way of talking out his feelings.

Theo rubbed his chin, the stubble making a raspy sound against his fingers. "I don't really have anyone, any... man, to bounce this off of."

Charlie appreciated his candor and felt honored that he was even considered for such a role. "Well, I may not have had the privilege of marrying or having children, but I've always been a pretty good listener." Theo sat quietly a moment, the truck bumping along at a slower pace than before, as if reaching their destination would end the important conversation too soon. Charlie didn't mind. Clearly the young man needed a father figure to talk to. He'd never considered himself to be such a man, but age-wise, he could see how he fit the bill. He also knew that this was a conversation that should have been Jerry's, and he felt guilty a moment for being the one to receive it, but he was here. Jerry wasn't. All he could do was his best at helping Theo out. He respected the young man. He also respected Jerry and Billy Lou enough to give him all the time he needed to get the words out, and he'd honor them by trying to give him the best advice he could think of.

"I think I'm just a bit nervous about the whole merging two lives part. She has her career, I have mine. She has Clare, who still has a few years of high school left. I even thought I wouldn't consider marriage until after Clare graduated because I didn't want her to have to adjust to something so new when she's about to leave the nest, so to speak. I also don't want to mess up the dynamic they have. They're two peas in a pod. I know their time together is special to Reesa, and she only has Clare under her roof a few more years. I don't want to interrupt their time together." Theo looked at Charlie briefly, his face showing slight traces of embarrassment at sharing such personal thoughts, but his eyes also pleading for an opinion other than his own. "But then there is the other side of me that just wants them now. I want Reesa as my wife, and I want Clare to have a father who cares about her and is willing to help her. I just don't know what to do or what my next move should be."

"Have you talked marriage with Reesa, yet?"

"No. I've been a bit... chicken in bringing it up."

Smiling, Charlie nodded. "I could see that being hard to do. You both have a lot you're riskin'.

"I don't feel like I'm risking much, just my peace. I'll never have a quiet moment if I marry Reesa." His lips twitched and Charlie could tell he didn't quite mind that possibility.

"Trust me, quiet is overrated anyway. There is such a thing as too much quiet. I would know."

They pulled alongside the ditch, and up ahead was an overgrown fence row and an old 1951 Ford pickup. "Well now, hello beautiful." Charlie whistled under his breath as they both hopped out of the truck and walked towards the rusty vehicle. Charlie ran his palm over the bumpy hood, and his excited smile had Theo grinning at him.

"I'll get some wire cutters." He marched back towards his truck toolbox as Charlie continued his survey of his newest treasure.

"Just what I need, another project." Charlie shook his head. "But this one looks pretty good. A quick one. We'll see what's under the hood once we pull it out, but I feel the thrill of it already. And that's a good sign."

Theo bent to his knees to look under the truck. "No boulders in the way. Just the fence and brambles, looks like."

A whimper touched the air and the two men looked at each other before both dropping to their knees to peer under the truck again. A small, brown ball of fur with sticker burrs, leaves, and twigs rustled from behind the front tire and the curve of the ditch, and two pale golden eyes looked up. Charlie's heart all but burst in delight. "A puppy!"

Theo laughed. "Oh boy." The younger man slid towards the front of the truck and reached underneath, his large hand scooping the mangy pup out from under the truck. He handed it to Charlie.

"Oh, man. Little thing is starvin' to death." Charlie hugged it closer, and the puppy squirmed to snuggle as close to Charlie as possible. "Are there more?"

Theo looked under the truck. "Looks like there may have been a couple more, but they didn't make it."

"Poor thing." Charlie held the puppy up and looked it over. "It's alright, sugar." He lifted the tail and confirmed the puppy was, in fact, a girl. "That's going to be your name. Sugar. And I'm going to keep you."

"Well, that didn't take much convincing. I thought I was going to have to convince Reesa or Billy Lou they had a new dog." Theo chuckled.

"Nope. This gal's mine. I need some company at that old house. Oh—" his face fell a moment.

Theo waved away his concern. "You can have her at my place. Trooper might be a little crazy at first, but she can live there too."

Charlie immediately tucked her back into his elbow. "Come on, Sugar, let's get you in the truck." He walked her towards Theo's truck, Theo reaching into his toolbox and removing an old woven blanket that Trooper typically laid on when he rode with him. Charlie set it on the floorboard and placed the puppy on it. She burrowed under the blanket and peered up at him. He gently petted her head. "That's a girl. We'll only be a minute." He shut the door and went back to work.

Chapter Seven

Billy Lou dumped the metal tub of dirty water outside over the back fence and glanced up at Reesa as she swept the back porch for the third time that day. "It doesn't look as sad, I guess."

Jason Wright's head popped into view of the broken back bedroom window. "You ladies are doing great!" He grinned before ducking back into the room to keep laying the groundwork for his restoration.

"I could go for some coffee," Reesa admitted. "I feel like my early morning is starting to catch up to me."

A happy toot of the horn had them both walking to the side of the house to see Jamie's car pulling up. "Does she have a sixth sense?" Reesa asked and turned surprised eyes on Billy Lou.

"God, I hope so." Billy Lou and Reesa waited patiently as Jamie slipped out of her car, both women briefly disappointed until Jamie held up her finger and reached back inside, withdrawing a cup carrier and a brown bag of treats.

"There she is," Reesa whispered in thankfulness.

"Honey, you are a life saver!" Billy Lou called.

"We literally *just* said the word coffee and you honked your horn."

Jamie laughed, her red curls bouncing as she walked across the yard. "The coffee beans sing to me, what can I say?" She handed Billy Lou a warm cup, Reesa an iced latte, and called, "Jason?"

His head popped up in the open window frame. "Yes ma'am?" His shoulders relaxed when he saw it was Jamie. "Well, hey there, pretty lady."

Jamie's cheeks flamed as red as her hair as she held up an extra coffee. "Want a coffee?"

"If you made it, you know it." He extended his hand out of the window and Jamie walked it over. She nervously handed it to him. "Want to come see my project?"

Jamie's eyes widened a moment. "Oh, sure. Okay." She turned towards the other women as he disappeared back into the room and pointed a hand to herself. "Me," she whispered. "He wants to show me." She softly giggled in excitement as she slipped into the house. Their voices could be heard through the open windows, and Jamie's appreciative response and wonder at the hole in the ground was just what Jason was after. She asked questions and they engaged in friendly banter back and forth.

"I think that's the most that girl has ever spoken to him in all her years on this earth," Billy Lou whispered.

"I know." Reesa smiled. "I'm kind of in shock."

"As am I..." Billy Lou's voice trailed off and Reesa leaned in her direction to see what had captured her attention. Theo's truck pulling up the drive with Charlie beside him and another rusted pickup behind it had Billy Lou stiffening. "That fool." She marched towards the truck, and as soon as Charlie stepped out, Billy Lou lit into him. "What on earth, Charlie Edwards? You already have a truck you're workin' on, and a house! Why did you even pick this junk up?"

Charlie grinned and then looked at Theo. "I got somethin' else too, Billy. Just you wait and see." He reached into the truck and withdrew the puppy. "Her name's Sugar. What'cha think?"

"A dog? You got a dog?" Billy Lou shook her head in dismay, but her hand briefly brushed over the puppy's fur. "Filthy little thing, isn't she?"

"She was under the truck. Only one of her litter

that survived being dumped there, I guess."

Billy Lou's countenance fell as sympathy took over. "Well, bless her heart. Let me see her." She handed Charlie her coffee cup and scooped the puppy into her arms. "Definitely needs a good scrubbin'. Looks like she may have some mange; the vet will take care of that. And food. Bless her heart, I can feel her sweet little ribs. Charlie," She swatted him. "why didn't you bring her to me at once?" She hurried the puppy towards Reesa and the two women began chatting.

"Well, I may have gotten and lost a puppy all in one day," Charlie murmured to Theo and the young man cleared his throat.

"Grandma, that's Charlie's puppy, you know?"

"Of course I know that. But he's busy, and by the looks of it *too* busy to be making vet trips and bathing puppies. I'll handle this one." She tucked the puppy in her arms and stroked its head. Jamie and Jason appeared on the front steps and Billy Lou admired them a moment. In an odd way, they'd fit rather nicely together, she thought. Jason's good looks and fit frame with Jamie's vivacious red hair, curves, and enthusiasm. She pondered it a moment longer before Jamie came to see what she was holding.

"This yours, Mr. Charlie?" Jamie bounced the puppy in her arms like an infant now, lightly tickling its belly. "She sure is cute."

"And what do you have there?" Reesa nodded towards the truck with a sly wink at him.

"I think this is Clare's future pickup."

"Oh?" Reesa looked at him and then the truck. "You going to tell her that?"

"No. I'm going to tell Teddy Graham that."

"Oh boy." Reesa laughed. "That poor boy."

"Guarantee I'll have that pickup fixed up real quick."

"Charlie, it's not right to play with that sweet boy's affections," Billy Lou scolded.

Jason grinned at the current conversation. "Ms. Billy Lou, that young man would serve his heart to Clare on the finest china if he could muster up the courage. This gives him an outlet to do just that."

"Not sure how I feel about that," Reesa mumbled, though she accepted the comforting arm over her shoulders from Theo. "But she would love it. And I've been saving some money back for a vehicle for her, so maybe that could go towards the project."

"No, no, no." Billy Lou shook her head. "Clare needs something reliable. Not something that's going to break down every five minutes."

"It wouldn't after I'm done with it." Charlie, offended, looked straight at Billy Lou.

She huffed. "No offense, but a young girl needs a car that is easy to maintain. A classic Ford pickup is just a disaster waiting to happen. What if she's out and about and the transmission blows? She can't just pull into the nearest dealership and ask them to fix it. It'd be a long, drawn-out process because it's a hot rod."

"Well, she does know a mechanic." Theo pointed at himself.

"And what about when she's off at college, Theodore. Are you going to be moving down there with her? Holding her hand?"

"Maybe," he muttered, and Reesa squeezed his side appreciatively.

"What do you think?" Reesa looked up at Theo and Billy Lou watched as they silently made the decision together.

"I think Clare's got herself a new pickup." Theo reached a hand out to Charlie and the latter shook it.

"I'll see if I can get it taken apart over the next couple of days and see what it's going to take. If I need to, I'll push the other project aside for now and just focus on this one." Charlie nodded that he liked the idea too.

"Y'all beat anything I've ever seen." Billy Lou shook her head in defeat.

"Uh oh. Now she's going to go buy a car for Clare out of fear and determination," Theo warned.

Billy Lou's eyes cut towards her grandson,

and he had the good sense to look apologetic. "No, Theodore, I'm not. I'm taking that puppy to the vet to get her a look over and a bath. I am then going to take her home and feed her. Or have you two men not noticed she's half starvin' by now?"

"We did." Theo's response was hesitant as his grandmother accepted the puppy back from Jamie. "Thanks for the coffee, honey. And since I'm making a trip to Hot Springs, have you ordered you a suit yet, Charlie?"

"A suit?"

"For the gala," Billy Lou reminded him.

"Oh."

"That's a no. Get in the car, Charlie." She pointed to her vehicle and his panicked face looked from one person to another.

Jamie giggled. "Best get going, Mr. Charlie. When Billy Lou's on a mission, there's no stoppin' her."

He looked longingly at the old pickup on the back of Theo's truck.

"I'll get it unloaded," Theo promised him with a smirk.

Billy Lou honked and Charlie's back stiffened. "I'm comin', Billy!" he barked. "Stop your nonsense!" He marched towards her car and opened the passenger door to Billy Lou scolding him not to dirty up the interior of her car with his dirty boots.

"Not sure if they'll make it to Hot Springs before one kills the other," Jason commented.

Jamie guffawed. "Oh, Ms. Billy has that man wrapped around her little finger, doesn't she? But I don't think Charlie realizes yet that he has the same with her."

"You think so?" Reesa asked.

"Oh yeah," Theo and Jamie said at the same time.

Surprised, Reesa looked up at Theo. "You think she likes him?"

"I do. I think she's struggling with it, but I think she does."

Reesa and Jamie squealed together.

"Uh oh." Jason laughed. "I sense some matchmaking wheels turning."

"Oh, they've been turning," Theo explained.

"So, Jason," Reesa looked at the good-looking carpenter. "you graduated with Theo and Jamie, right?"

"I did," he replied, his hands on his hips above his tool belt. "Why?"

"Are you going to the high school reunion?"

"Ah." His cheeks flushed. "I don't know about that."

"Why not?" Reesa asked. "We're all going."

His face lit up a moment. "Theo?" His surprise was

evident, and Theo shrugged.

"I was out voted."

"You could join us," Reesa invited. "We could all go to dinner beforehand and then hang out at the reunion for however long Theo lasts."

That comment made Jamie laugh and elbow Theo in the side. "She's got you pegged, doesn't she, T.J.?"

Jason smiled in response, and he looked from one face to another. "Well, I guess if y'all don't mind another one to tag along, that sounds like it might be fun."

"Not at all." Reesa looked up at Theo and beamed. "Once we figure out a game plan, I'll send you the details." She turned her attention back to the building beside them. "The house awaits."

"I've got an hour." Jamie clapped her hands together. "Put me to work, girl." And she enthusiastically jumped right into helping.

^

"I haven't worn a suit in a long time." Charlie shifted uncomfortably under the tailor's watchful eye as the man penciled here and there along his shoulders. "Is this all really necessary? There are suits on the rack."

"No. You need a fitted suit. This is the type of affair you have to look your best."

"I can look my best in a cheaper suit." He looked at the tailor. "No offense." The young man softly smiled as he continued his work, as if he felt sympathy for Charlie's losing battle and had witnessed it a hundred times before. His hands never wavered in his work. "And what about you?" Charlie challenged. "Are you getting fitted for your dress? It's only fair."

"I already have my dress. And yes, it was fitted to me. I come here every year. Don't I, Timothy?" she asked the young man. He nodded silently and she looked pleased. A little too pleased, Charlie thought.

He shifted again slightly and flinched, a pin poking him in the shoulder.

"If you hold still, Timothy could get done and we could go get some lunch."

"I'd like to get back to the house. I have people working on it, without pay, and I feel guilty for not being there too."

"They're helping because they want to."

"I know that." Charlie consciously tried to stand as still as possible so Timothy could finish quickly. "I just feel like I should pay them for all the help."

"They wouldn't want it. Accept the help, Charlie."

"But—"

"No buts. We take care of our people here in Piney."

"Oh, so I'm one of the people of Piney now, am I? I thought I was the scum of the earth Charlie Edwards."

Billy Lou's lips flattened. "I don't recall anyone saying that."

"But you have definitely thought it."

"Well, that's before I knew."

"Knew what?"

"Your circumstances."

"Ah, so you find out my daddy was an alcoholic and now you have some sympathy, hm?"

Billy Lou sighed. "Are you wanting to argue?"

"No. Just trying to figure you out, Billy. You treated me like a jerk the first week I was here, then you start helping me on my house, without being asked, and now you're making me dress up in a suit for some charity thing—all within a two week time span—and I'm just trying to figure out if you still hate me or if you are just tolerating me because Theo likes me. I can't figure you out."

"I don't hate you," Billy Lou admitted.

"Really?" He looked doubtful, but he saw her eyes soften a bit.

"Really." She lifted her gaze to his. "You just sometimes make me sad."

"Because I'm Jerry's age and I'm not him." He'd hit

the nail on the head and he could tell. Timothy expertly excused himself.

"Don't say that."

"Why, when it's the truth?"

"Because it's not your fault he's not here. It's not my fault either. It's just... he's not. And I have to accept it, even if I don't want to. Even if it takes every ounce of my strength some days. So yes, I'm sad when I look at you. Because when I do have moments of fun with you, I think I'm being unfair. I'm being disloyal. And that it isn't fair that Jerry isn't here. It's not fair at all. And when I see you active, thriving, and chummy with Theodore, it hurts me. Not because you're doing anything wrong. You're not. It's just that it makes me miss Jerry. Because that's what Jerry would and should be doing."

"You're right. It's not fair." Charlie knelt in front of her and grabbed her hands in his. To his surprise, she let him. "I'm sorry you lost Jerry, Billy. He was a golden guy. Yes, I didn't know him after high school, but based on you and Theo and the people around you loving him the way y'all do, it tells me that he was a stand-up guy. And he loved you, but I don't think he'd be upset with you for being happy when he's not here. He wouldn't want you to be sad. It's not fair to weigh my living against his passing. I'm going to die too one day. That's part of life. He didn't do it to make you upset, it was just his time."

She swiped a tear that spilled over her cheek, and he reached into his back pocket for his handkerchief and handed it to her. She dabbed her face. "I know all that," she mumbled. "I just struggle with it."

"I imagine you do." He squeezed her hand. "I'm actually quite envious of you."

"Why on earth would you envy my grief?" She looked perplexed and on the verge of anger.

"Because you loved someone that much. I've never had that in my life. Ever. And I can't even imagine being loved like that. You're a precious gift, Billy Lou Waldrup. And Jerry Whitley recognized that fact early on. I'd love to have a love like you two did. It wasn't in the cards for me."

"Don't say that." Billy Lou swiped her face again.

Charlie smirked. "Well, God sure would have a sense of humor if it happened to me at this age. I'm not upset with Him. I've lived my life, and I'm grateful for every day of it. But you, Billy, man... you and Jerry created a beautiful family and a beautiful life together. I feel rather lucky getting to enjoy parts of it now. Your grandson, Reesa, Clare, Jamie. All of you have been a breath of fresh air for me the last couple of weeks, so thank you for that." He slowly stood to his feet. "Now, let me get pricked and prodded some more so we can get out of here and get some lunch. Because part of me doesn't like this whole shopping thing, and the other part of me actually wants to go back to that old house and enjoy it with the people that are there. And trust me, I've never wanted to go back to that old house before now."

Billy Lou stood to her feet and squared her shoulders. Her eyes, though still glassy, held a resolute determination of doing her best to climb out of her current wave of grief, and his respect for her grew even more. "You're a strong one, Billy, and I grow more and more impressed with you by the day. Just want you to know that."

Her lips quivered a moment before she motioned for Timothy to step back into the space and finish his work. "Don't think that sweet talkin' me is going to get you out of this dinner, Charlie Edwards."

His lips quirked at the corners, and he nodded. "I wouldn't dream of it."

"Good. I'm going to look at cuff links." She walked away, slinging her purse over her shoulder. He liked that she took the time she needed to finish pulling herself together. He also liked that they were able to have an open and candid conversation about their feelings. He couldn't recall ever doing that with anyone. He appreciated her honesty about her grief. And though he didn't understand the depth of it, he respected it and valued her. He hoped, over time, she'd see just how much.

Chapter Eight

Billy Lou relaxed against the oversized massage chair and relished the feel of the warm water soaking her feet. Reesa sat to her right and Jamie to her left doing the same. "You girls have your outfits picked for tonight?"

"Yes ma'am." Reesa nodded. "Clare helped me choose."

"What's the dress?"

"Cocktail attire," Jamie replied with an eyeroll.

"You wearing that pretty black dress you usually wear to the charity functions with me?" she asked Jamie.

"No. I was under strict orders that I had to buy a new dress." She looked at Reesa. "And I'm glad I did, even though I despise dress shopping."

Billy Lou chuckled. "Well, I'd take you dress shopping any day over taking Charlie to be fitted for a suit again. That man squirmed more than a teenage boy after curfew."

"Oh yeah, how was that yesterday?" Reesa looked intrigued. "I wasn't able to ask all the nosey questions when he got back to the house because he and Theo immediately started talking about the new truck project."

"It was fine. We got him a nice suit."

"That's it?" Jamie looked disappointed.

"What else would there be?" Billy Lou laughed. "We went to get him a suit. We got him a suit." She waved her hands from one point to the other.

"Did he look handsome in it?"

"If he hadn't been covered in mud from his truck extrication earlier, he would have, yes. I'll think he'll look very nice tonight, if he remembers his schedule and gives himself plenty of time to clean up."

"Are you nervous?" Reesa asked.

"Why would I be nervous?"

"Well, you have a date. I'm assuming this is your first date since Mr. Jerry passed away, right?"

Billy Lou quieted a moment. She hadn't quite considered the event with Charlie as a potential date. "I hadn't thought of it like that."

"Well, let's face it, he's not me." Jamie fluffed her hair on a giggle. "So don't get your hopes up, Billy Lou. I'm hard to beat."

"That you are, my girl." Billy Lou grinned and patted Jamie's hand next to her. "Guess I will have to hand you off to the handsome Mr. Wright for the evening."

Jamie's face blanched. "We're not going together."

"Sure you are. Theodore and Reesa will be together, and you will be with Jason."

Jamie looked at Reesa's pleased smile and her jaw dropped. "How did you do it?" She pointed at her friend and narrowed her eyes. "How did I not see you were setting me up?"

"It's a gift." Reesa shrugged her shoulders and laughed. "It was actually Theo's idea, believe it or not."

"No way. T.J. would never recommend Jason Wright for anything. The man's existence drives T.J. nuts."

"He's coming around," Reesa explained. "After Jason helped me with the pergola project, Theo realized he wasn't as bad as his reputation made him out be. I mean, he's still a little weirded out by the whole married three times and divorced bit, but he thinks Jason is nice enough. And that's a start."

"I'm sure Jason doesn't see it as a date either. We're going as a group," Jamie asserted, convinced that was the most plausible explanation.

"Or maybe he agreed because he doesn't mind the thought of taking you on a hot date," Reesa suggested with a sly smile.

Jamie shook her head, her red curls bouncing as she did so. "No way. Trust me. I'm not... his usual type."

"Nothing wrong with that. Sometimes a man doesn't know what he needs until it hits him right in the face." Billy Lou nodded towards Reesa as an example.

"More like *sprays* him in the face. Hey, I could loan you my pepper spray," she offered Jamie.

The women laughed.

"Let's not go that far... yet." Jamie giggled.

"We are still getting ready at your house, right Billy Lou?" Reesa asked.

"Yes ma'am. Will Clare be coming to help us?"

"She plans to. My dad is going to come up and spend the evening with her. I think they plan to go to a movie and eat out. He mentioned that maybe my mom would join them." Reesa's voice wavered at the last part.

"And how does Clare feel about that? Better yet, how do you feel about that?" Jamie asked.

"Not sure. Dad thinks it might be easier for her to ease back into the idea of us in her life if it's just Clare to start."

"Hurtful," Billy Lou commented.

"Yeah... I'm trying not to let it bother me, but it kind of does. At the same time, maybe he's right. I told Clare it was up to her. I also told her that if my mom joins them, she will not go alone and that she needs to invite a friend. Of course, Teddy was first on the list, which, I'm glad of, because he knows the whole situation. Dad has met him before and likes him. And I trust him with Clare."

"Big words, right there." Jamie exhaled a heavy breath.

"I know." Reesa tenderly smiled. "He is a great kid. And he treats Clare with respect and kindness. What more could I ask for in a friend for her?"

"Annnnnnd he's scared of Theo," Jamie added.

"That helps too." Reesa beamed with pride and Billy Lou chuckled.

"Half this town is scared of Theodore for some odd reason," Billy Lou added.

"Um, probably because he was an anti-social mountain man when Reesa arrived," Jamie explained.

"And he only communicated in grunts and growls," Reesa continued. "Though, now I find those kind of cute."

Billy Lou reached over and patted her hand on a chuckle. "I'm glad you do. And I'm glad you saw through that scruff to the gem he is underneath." She eased back into her chair and closed her eyes as the massage chair gently rolled up and down her back and the nail attendant stroked deep purple polish over her toenails.

"So do you think the men are as worked up over this evening as we are?" Jamie asked.

"I'm not worked up," Reesa said.

"Well, you don't have to be. You didn't go to school with all the people you'll be meeting tonight." Jamie sighed. "I'm glad T.J. decided to go to this one. It was hard last time when he wasn't there. We're misfits together. My compañero was missing. It was weird. And I didn't have anyone to really talk to, nor did anyone really try to talk to me."

"Was Jason there?"

"Yes, but he was married at the time, so they were mingling amongst his old friends. Which... Jason was like Theo... they had *lots* of friends."

"Theodore had acquaintances. I wouldn't say he had friends," Billy Lou clarified.

"True," Jamie agreed. "Jason, however, would claim most of our class as friends."

"Well, that'll be neat tonight then." Reesa motioned towards her. "Especially if you two show up together. I bet the tongues will wag." She winked and Jamie flashed a panicked look at Billy Lou.

Offering a calm pat to the young woman's hand, she shook her head. "You just have fun, honey. Don't focus on the others. Enjoy a night out with your friends. Don't read too much into Jason. He's going to have fun as well. Nothing to stress over. And *you*—" Billy Lou pointed at Reesa. "stop your matchmaking, missy."

Reesa held up both hands in surrender. "I'll do my best."

"Alright, Ms. Billy Lou, you're all set." The young woman at her feet stood up. "You want to sit for a bit to let them dry? Or you can come to the chair over here." She motioned across the room and Billy Lou shook her head. "I'll just sit right here, Tammy, until the girls are finished too. Thank you, honey." The woman quietly walked away.

Reesa's phone buzzed next to her, and she held up the picture Clare had sent to her. "Seems like the cat is out of the bag." Clare's excited face in a selfie with a serious-faced Theo and a grinning Charlie filled her phone screen. "*Theo's excited too,*" Reesa read and then laughed, gently rubbing a finger over her boyfriend's stoic face. "Gotta love him."

"So, she now knows she's got a vehicle lined up. I thought y'all were going to keep it secret?" Billy Lou asked.

"I guess she bugged them enough. She has a knack knack for that. It's inherited... from me." Reesa grinned. "That's a great picture, too." She held up her phone again and typed a quick message to her daughter. "I'm so thankful for all the people in my daughter's life. She has more love surrounding her here in Piney than she's ever had."

"Y'all just needed to find where you fit." Billy Lou pointed to her and Jamie. "And with us and Piney, you do."

"Well, I do think I will forever be indebted to the both of you. To you, Billy Lou, for allowing Clare and I to rent the cabin and giving us a place to live here in Piney. And to you, Jamie, for openly embracing me and pushing me to act on my feelings for Theo."

"I think you and Theo will forever be my best work," Jamie squealed.

"Speaking of work," Billy Lou reached into her purse and withdrew a white tea towel. "while I'm waiting for you two girls to finish your pedicures, I'm going to work on my latest project."

"What's that?" Reesa asked.

"I'm making Clare her own set," Billy Lou explained. "With images from Piney." She held up the one she was working on. "This one is of Trooper. Well, to the best of my abilities it will be of Trooper. Those two are soul mates. I just finished one with a little cabin on the front." She smoothed the fabric on her lap and tightened her stitching ring. "I plan to edge them with some pretty floral touches too, but right now, I'm focusing on the bigger images. It's been a while since I've cross stitched, so I'm having to pace myself... and not lose my temper at all the mistakes I make and have to redo."

"She is going to absolutely love those, Billy Lou."

"I thought it might be special for her." Billy Lou squeezed Reesa's hand. "You two have brought a lot of light and joy into Theodore's life, and mine!"

"And mine!" Jamie chirped.

"Ditto." Reesa leaned her head back and closed her eyes. They popped open immediately with the dawning of a new idea. "You know, they should really make a movie about all of us."

Billy Lou hooted in laughter. "Why on earth should there be a movie about us?"

"I think we make good stories."

"You just want to see Theo up on a big screen," Jamie challenged.

"Well, that wouldn't hurt, would it?" Reesa wiggled her eyebrows.

"Close your eyes and relax." Billy Lou shooed the thought away.

"She can't now. She's thinking about Theo on the silver screen."

Without opening her eyes, Reesa smiled. "Mmhmm."

^

Charlie stretched his shoulders. He had to admit it, Timothy cut a good suit. And he also had to admire that he didn't look half bad wearing it. It'd been at least three decades since he'd worn a suit, and he liked that he didn't feel stuffed into a penguin costume like he had the first time he wore one. He straightened his tie, the deep plum color supposedly matching the color of Billy Lou's dress. She'd helped him pick the tie, so it was obviously close enough to appease her tastes. It wasn't really fair that she'd seen him in his suit and he had yet to see her dress, but he assumed that was just how life worked. Women liked the dramatic reveal part of a night out. He'd imagine Billy Lou looking beautiful, because she naturally always was. She always dressed neatly, stylishly, and with flare. Her hair was always fixed, her nails always painted, and her lips always some shade of color. He expected the typical Billy Lou, all put together. He looked at himself in the mirror one more time and then headed out into the main living area of Theo's house, the younger man patiently waiting on him so that they could ride together. Theo was dressed in slacks and a starched button up shirt.

"Well, now, how do you get by without having to wear one of these?" Charlie waved a hand over his full suit.

"I'm not going with Billy Lou."

Charlie harrumphed, walked over to the refrigerator, and withdrew a small clear box holding a fresh corsage. He saw Theo's surprise. "Isn't this what you're supposed to do for these types of things?"

Theo smirked. "Now, you're just making me look bad."

Charlie chuckled and walked over to make sure his new puppy was content with Trooper as her housemate. He scratched beneath her chin, her soulful eyes looking up at him in adoration. Trooper's tail thumped and he gave him a good scratch as well. Assured that Sugar and Trooper would stay out of trouble, he followed Theo out the door.

They arrived to find an awaiting Clare eagerly hopping from one foot to another. She squealed when they emerged from Theo's truck. "Theo!" She circled around him and then slapped him on the shoulder. "Look at you! Mom's going to flip! Did you trim your beard too?" She laughed as she jumped to hug him. "And Mr. Charlie," She studied him in his suit. "you look fantastic!"

"You're going to make me blush, sweetheart."

Clare beamed as Jason's truck pulled to a stop in front of Billy Lou's. He wore similar styled clothing to Theo, but in shades of blue, his navy slacks stark against the bright green grass.

"Whoa," Clare murmured, the other two men eyeing her curiously. "What? He's cute." She shrugged her shoulders and waved at him as he approached. "As good as you look, I'm afraid to tell you that the women have you beat." Clare's smile lifted even higher when Teddy's truck pulled up, her grandfather riding shotgun. Roger Tate stepped out, his face lit with a smile upon seeing his granddaughter and Theo. He shook hands with Theo and then introduced himself to Jason and Charlie.

"I was over at Reesa's when Teddy showed up. I'd about given up on you." He hugged Clare tightly.

"Sorry, I forgot I'd be over here. I meant to text you. Glad you figured it out." She playfully punched Teddy's arm.

"Clare!" Jamie's voice called from the house, and she snapped her fingers. "Oops, sorry, I forgot my role. I have to go do a final look over before they come out here." She hurried back into the house.

"You guys..." She shut the door and leaned against it fanning herself. "The men look on fire."

Reesa nudged her daughter out of the way and peeked out the front window. "Oh. She's not lying."

"Well, then, I guess we should not keep them waiting." Billy Lou opened the door and stepped out first, her plum dress billowing behind her.

"Dramatic much?" Jamie whispered with glee, following behind her.

Charlie watched as Billy Lou walked up the sidewalk towards him. She was breathtaking, her long dress flowing behind her as she gracefully walked. She turned to face towards her house as Reesa and Jamie emerged as well.

Theo straightened his shoulders as Reesa approached with a wide smile and wearing a sleek black dress that accentuated her curves. She whistled when she approached him. "Look at you." She circled him just as Clare had, and Theo shifted uncomfortably on his feet. She laughed as she linked her arm with his and stood on her tiptoes to kiss him. "I like you all fixed up."

"Ditto," Theo murmured, his eyes sharp as he stared down at her and soaked her in.

Jamie only had a brief second of awkwardness before Jason stepped forward with a single rose just for her. "I figured if they're partnered up, maybe that meant we were. If you would do me the pleasure, Jamie?" He extended the rose, and she nervously took it.

"Oh, s-s-sure. I don't mind." She flashed a shy smile and Jason nodded in approval.

"Well, time is of the essence," Billy Lou called out.

"Do we all turn into pumpkins at midnight?" Reesa asked.

"Probably just Theo," Clare teased, elbowing him in the side and grinning when he scowled at her.

"You two behave," he warned. "I've got eyes and ears everywhere."

Teddy and Clare both laughed nervously and Reesa rolled her eyes. "Have fun." She gave her dad a hug. "Don't let them talk you into a double feature, Dad. They're bad about that." She tousled Teddy's hair before giving Clare a big hug. "We'll be back late. Just stay here at Billy Lou's after supper until I get back."

"Yes ma'am."

Charlie listened as plans were made and confirmed for the young people, but he watched Billy Lou sort through her clutch purse and double check that she had everything she needed. She honestly had no idea she was so stunning. He shifted and realized he still held the corsage in his hands. "Oh," He stepped towards her. "I... I got you this to wear, if you'd like." He held up the clear box and Billy Lou's eyes bounced between it and him. "If it doesn't go with your look, I understand. I'm a bit out of practice at these sorts of things."

Billy Lou accepted the box and opened it. A white rose with small wisps of baby's breath were encased in white ribbon. "It's lovely." Billy Lou handed him the box and then extended her hand. The diamond bracelet around her delicate wrist sparkled in the setting sun. He clumsily hurried to remove the corsage and gently slipped it on to her hand. She admired it a moment longer and then handed him her car keys. "Ready?"

"When you are." Charlie heaved a relieved sigh at finally heading towards her sleek SUV and out of the spotlight of the younger adults. He opened the passenger door for her as she slid in and adjusted the bottom of her dress so as not to wrinkle or get it caught in the door. On her signal, he closed her in. He offered a final wave towards the group and hopped behind the wheel.

"I feel like I'm watching my grandma go to prom," Theo commented.

"Kind of feels like it, hm?" Reesa smiled up at him. "How do you feel about Charlie being her escort?"

"Not as weird about it as I thought I would."

"That's good," she whispered. "because I think Billy Lou was excited too."

Theo tugged her closer to his side. "But right now, I want to go to my high school reunion and show off my beautiful girlfriend."

Her brows lifted. "Oh really?"

"Why not? I haven't done a lot of things right in my life, Reesa. But you... well, you're right."

Her face grew serious before she planted a soft, and intimate kiss to his lips.

Clare cleared her throat. "Ooooooookay. I think it's time you all get going. Have her home by midnight, Theo."

Roger Tate chuckled at his daughter's curfew

order and Theo just smirked her direction.

"Likewise," Theo mentioned to Teddy about Clare, and the young man saluted him in understanding.

They all piled into Jason's truck and set off for a night down memory lane.

Chapter Nine

The Hot Springs National Park Convention Center lit up before them as Charlie signalled his turn to enter the parking lot. Valets rushed from car to car as people flooded the entrance. Billy Lou's heart raced. She always grew anxious before big events, though most people didn't know that. But seeing the beautiful gowns, the majestic glow of the lights, and the reflective windows showcasing the night sky, she felt those familiar butterflies.

"My goodness, people really come out for this, don't they?" Charlie's voice interrupted her thoughts and she nodded.

"It will be crowded, that's for certain."

"You come to this every year?"

"I do."

"And they're raising funds for what?"

"CHI St. Vincent's Hospital has incredible pediatric care throughout the city. This gala helps support those clinics. Most of the hospital's major funding goes towards its cancer treatment programs and the neurosciences. By helping fund the children's clinics, we're ensuring the children receive the best of care in pediatrics available."

"And why is this important to you?" Charlie asked curiously.

"All my grandbabies were born in Hot Springs. Care back then wasn't near what it is today, but there were some rough times. NICU for months with Theodore, believe it or not. It was dreadful. The staff was wonderful, and the facilities at the time were as up to date as they could have been then. But my heart just went out to all those families, especially the ones that were there for months at a time. Some of this funding goes straight toward housing those families so they do not have to drive back and forth from home, wherever that may be. I was also a nurse for thirty years."

Charlie turned to her in surprise. "Really?"

Billy Lou smiled. "Why are you so shocked?"

"I just didn't know." Charlie waited in line for the

valet. "I guess I just assumed you didn't work outside the home."

"Well, I did that too."

"Billy Lou Waldrup became a nurse." His voice quieted. "I could see that. You're great with people and you have this fire in you when you're determined to help somebody."

"And how would you know that?"

He pointed at himself. "Do you not recall bossing me around the last two weeks?" His lips tilted upward when her face blanched. "Seriously?"

"Bossing? I'd never." Billy Lou let the comment linger a moment before they both started laughing. "I guess you're right, but don't act like you haven't enjoyed having all the help."

"I won't deny that," Charlie admitted. "You've got a great group of people in your life, Billy. That grandson of yours has a decent head on his shoulders, the woman he loves is a gem, and her daughter is probably one of the best kids I've ever met. And Jamie is a pure delight. Not sure if we had people like that in Piney back in the day, but I wasn't aware of them if we did, so my experience this go around is much better than the first eighteen years of my life. And I'm enjoying getting to know everyone."

They reached the drop off and Charlie exited the vehicle first, waving away the valet from Billy Lou's door as he opened it himself. She appreciated the effort and accepted his hand to help her out of the car. When she stood, her dress billowed around her and draped just as she hoped it would. She loved her dress, and she hadn't worn such a style before, but she felt like a queen. Charlie offered his arm, and she tucked her hand into his elbow as they followed several others inside. The building was filled with elaborately decorated tables and floral arrangements, and people mingled around high tables for cocktails as the ceremony had yet to start.

"Where to?" Charlie leaned closer to her to whisper. Her grip on his arm tightened as she took a moment to catch her bearings. "They usually have a check-in table set up. Ah... there it is." She pointed and they made their way towards a long line of people standing to learn their table assignment. She felt Charlie fidget slightly and took a minute to study his profile. "You're staring." His hushed tone made her smile.

"I am." His eyes held a touch of amusement when he looked down at her. "Just checking to see how you're handling all this."

He patted her hand. "Like most things in my life, Billy, all in stride."

"You are pretty good at that, aren't you?"

"I'd like to think so." They shuffled forward a couple of steps and continued to wait. "Easiest way to live. No sense in getting worked up if things don't happen according to plan. Going with the flow tends to make me happier in the long run. I don't like to stress over things."

"Me either, though I will admit I stress too much over lots of things. Like Theodore, mostly. However, since Reesa's entered the picture, I have felt the majority of that stress disappear. He's taken care of and loved now, and that's what I've always wanted for him. Though, his hesitancy on popping the question to that girl has me stressing in a whole new way now."

"I wouldn't stress too much about that." Charlie smiled. "The wheels are turning for him. He's just sorting it all out and trying to figure out the best timing."

"Oh really?"

Charlie nodded.

"And he told you this, did he?"

"He did."

"Oh." Billy Lou was surprised Theodore would confide in Charlie over such a matter.

"Does it bother you?"

Gauging whether or not it did, Billy Lou shook her head. "No."

He narrowed his eyes a moment and she chuckled. "Honestly, it doesn't. Trust me. I was just fishing around in my mind and heart for whether or not it did, and surprisingly it does not bother me. I thought it would. Theodore needs another man to talk things out with, and with Jerry gone, he sought your counsel. It makes sense." They moved forward a couple of steps. "And as long as it was good counsel," She mimicked his narrowed eyes as she looked at him and he nodded. "then I'm okay with it."

"Mostly I just listened," Charlie explained. "Seems like that's all he really needed."

"Good. Theodore would be a fool to pass on Reesa."

"He won't," Charlie assured her. "She's a life changer, and those don't come along every day."

Billy Lou liked that term: *life changer*. She wondered if Jerry had felt that way about her.

"And before you ask, yes, you are a life changer gal too, Billy." He winked at her as they finally reached the table to check-in. She handed him his welcome pamphlet as she took her own and listened as the woman directed them to where their seats would be for the dinner. When they reached their table, several people were already seated, and curious eyes flew to Charlie's presence when they recognized Billy Lou.

"Evening," Billy Lou greeted warmly and then squealed in pure delight at one of the fellow tablemates who turned to look at the new arrivals. "Kathy?"

"Billy Lou Whitley! My goodness, it's been ages."

The woman stood and embraced Billy Lou, her eyes landing on Charlie behind her. "You look stunning." The woman admired her dress and Billy Lou thanked her profusely. "And this must be Charlie." The woman extended one hand to shake his and the other pointing to the name card on the table next to Billy Lou's. "Kathy Overton. Nice to meet you."

"Kathy and I both worked for Doctor Stephen Perkins for about a decade or so," Billy Lou explained to Charlie as he pulled her chair out from the table and waited patiently for her to adjust her dress to sit before finding his own chair. "How are you? How's John?" Billy Lou asked.

Kathy's face fell slightly, and she shook her head.

"I'm sorry to hear that, honey." Billy Lou patted her hand.

"It's been a little over a year since he passed," Kathy continued. "Hard to believe."

"I understand. Trust me."

"Yes. I know you do." Kathy, feeling relieved someone shared in similarity to her circumstances, faced her loss as bravely as she could. "I brought a dear friend of mine tonight. Kathy motioned to the man beside her and though he was engaged in conversation with the people on the other side of him, he immediately turned his attention to Kathy when she tapped his hand. "This is Billy Lou Whitley, the nurse I was telling you about."

"Ah." The man's face lit up and he nodded in greeting. "Denver Cole. Neo-neuro specialist."

Billy Lou's brow lifted slightly. "Well, nice to meet you, Dr. Cole. Are you a physician at CHI St. Vincent?"

He nodded. "Yes ma'am. Thank you for your support of the hospital."

"Of course." Billy Lou motioned towards Charlie. "This is Charlie Edwards. We go all the way back to our high school days and he just recently moved back to Piney."

Kathy's face lit into a bright smile. "Now, how about that? That's wonderful. Old flame? Reunited?" she asked, which had both Billy Lou and Charlie blushing and shaking their heads with an emphatic no.

"Just friends," Billy Lou commented, but when she turned to look at Charlie, her heart softened towards the handsome man beside her. He looked completely polished and put together, as if he attended such a soiree on a regular basis. But his eyes gave him away. She could sense a small touch of discomfort at being in such a setting and the thought of him attending because she'd asked him to made her appreciate him more. "He's been a good sport about me roping him into coming."

Kathy chuckled. "I understand, Charlie, completely."

Though Billy Lou imagined it was not difficult at all

for Kathy to enjoy coming, especially with a doctor almost two decades her junior, she appreciated her positive camaraderie.

"I am a willing participant tonight." Charlie flashed his charming smile Kathy's direction. "And I will gladly take Billy anywhere, especially when she looks as stunningly gorgeous as she does tonight." He turned his thousand-watt smile on her and she felt a small flutter around her heart.

"Well, you aren't wrong there. That dress is beyond remarkable, Billy Lou. It's absolutely stunning."

"Thank you," Billy Lou replied, though her attention was not on Kathy but on Charlie. Their gazes held a moment longer, both intrigued at an underlying buzz now floating between them. Kathy took the cue and bit back a smile as she briefly gave them a moment of privacy to converse with her date and the others at the table. A string quartet began to play at the front of the room as waiters appeared and began flooding the table with beverages. Billy Lou snapped her attention back to the moment and graciously thanked the young man who filled her glass. *What had just happened?* Her heart raced in her chest as she became even more deeply aware of Charlie's presence beside her and the way he'd made her feel with just a simple comment. *But he'd felt something too, hadn't he?* He'd held her eye straight on when she looked at him. She saw his hand move towards hers before she broke contact and interrupted the moment. *Would he have grabbed her hand and kissed it? Held it? Tugged her closer to whisper something sweet to her? And did she want him to?* That was the real burning question leaping around in her mind at the moment, because the answer was *yes*. She had wanted him to. And... she *wanted* him to. And though it warred with every ounce of her loyalty to Jerry, her good sense, and her evening plans, all she could think about was sharing another moment just like it with him again. *What had Charlie Edwards done to her?*

Charlie listened to the chatter and buzz of the convention center. Every table seemed to have the same friendly disposition his had, and he liked that people could come together for such a cause and actually enjoy the evening without being bored. A string quartet played in the background, though they were set up on the stage at the front. The waiter came to the table to offer glasses of wine. He politely declined. Billy Lou accepted the white and continued her conversation with Kathy. He watched as they reminisced over their time together and Billy Lou's face never once fell from a beautiful smile. Her hair was swooped back into a tight twist, the stark white strands looking almost blonde in the center's lights, and it was easy to envision her as that pretty high school girl he grew up knowing. She hadn't changed all that much in fifty years. And he had to admit, she was still the prettiest girl he'd ever met. The Billy Lou from the past was pretty, the Billy Lou of the present was a complete and total knockout. Life had seasoned her beauty with grace, and he felt as if he could stare at her forever and never grow tired of the view. Now, he knew that wasn't the polite thing to do, so he continued roaming his eyes about the room to avoid seeming too obvious. But he wanted to memorize this moment with her, memorize her in that dress, because he wasn't sure he'd ever seen anyone so beautiful, and he didn't want to forget it.

Her hand tapped his arm and she nodded towards the open floor area in front of the stage as couples began to dance to the music. He hoped she didn't want to dance. He was a terrible dancer. "That's new," Billy Lou commented. "They've never had a dance floor before."

"Are you going to show us how it's done, Billy Lou?" Kathy asked with a slight chuckle as she took a sip of her wine.

"Oh, heaven's no." Billy Lou waved away the suggestion. "I'm just pleasantly surprised is all."

"Last year, the night went longer than they expected, I think, and I guess they thought they needed something a little extra for those who lingered."

"Makes sense." Billy Lou turned her eyes on

Charlie. He wasn't watching her, but the couples softly swaying about the floor. He could feel her eyes studying him again and he turned to meet them. They briefly narrowed on him. "You okay?" she asked quietly.

He nodded in the affirmative and looked up as their dinner plates were brought to the table. Filet mignon, asparagus, and parmesan potato assortment were before him. It looked fantastic. He jolted in his chair a moment when he felt Billy Lou's delicate hand slide into his. She grinned at his surprise and then leaned her head towards his, her eyes closed as she whispered a quick prayer for their meal and the rest of their evening. When she finished, she squeezed his hand, but Charlie held onto it a moment longer. He lifted it to his lips and gave it a soft kiss before releasing it. Her cheeks bloomed in color before she turned back to her plate and began cutting into her meal. The meal was delicious, as he expected, but the night drifted at a snail's pace. By the third hour, Charlie was itching to head home. He wasn't sure how long the evening typically lasted, but his dissatisfaction almost became audible when Kathy talked of not leaving until midnight the previous year. It was nine and Charlie was reaching his tipping point. He'd attend as long as Billy Lou wished, but his discomfort grew by the minute. He excused himself and took a walk about the room. He paused to admire some of the silent auction items and just stood listening to the quartet continue to play.

"I don't know about you, but I think I'm about ready to wrap this up." Billy Lou's voice reached him before he felt her hand slide over his back in a comforting circle. He straightened. "Are you sure?"

"I am." She nodded. "I've talked. I've mingled. I've donated. I'm done." She grinned. "Let's sneak out while we have a chance."

"Are you sure?" Charlie asked again, motioning back towards their table.

"I'm sure. Kathy's been dancing with that doctor the last half hour. It's a nice time to slip out."

"Alright." Charlie offered her his arm and they made their way towards the exit. Relief seemed to hit both of them at the sight of the valet pulling her SUV towards the curb. Charlie opened her door and then walked around the hood to slide behind the wheel. "Well, was I a better date than Jamie?"

Billy Lou laughed. "You did quite well, and you lasted longer than I thought you would."

"Oh really? Thought I'd bail on ya, did you?"

"Let's just say I did not think you would stay so amiable throughout the evening once you were ready to leave."

"This evening wasn't about me," Charlie pointed out.

"No, it wasn't." Billy Lou smiled at him. "And you saying that is sweet. I'm glad you saw the importance of it." She sighed, closed her eyes, and leaned her head against the headrest of her seat.

"Don't go falling asleep on me now. I stayed awake all evening. It's only fair."

Her lips tilted into a smile, but her eyes remained closed. "I'm not drifting. I'm just relaxed. It's the wine. How do you not feel the same?"

"I didn't drink it," Charlie replied, turning onto the highway and grateful it wasn't a terribly long drive back to Piney.

"You didn't?" Billy Lou asked curiously.

"I don't drink, Billy,"he stated.

"Oh. Really?" Her interest piqued, she opened her eyes and looked at him. "For how long?"

"My whole life."

"Charlie Edwards, are you serious?"

"Yes."

"But in high school—"

"I had the reputation, I know." He rolled his eyes.

"But you didn't?"

"Nope. I smoked for a brief moment under the bleachers from about tenth to eleventh grade, but even that didn't stick."

"Interesting." Billy Lou studied him a moment. "Any particular reason why?"

He was sure she already knew, but he appeased her curiosity anyway. "When you grow up with an alcoholic, the appeal just isn't there. My biggest fear as a kid was turning into my dad. And if there was some way I could stop that from happening, I was going to do it. He was fine before he started drinking, therefore, in my young mind, that was the catalyst. If I could just stay away from alcohol, I'd be fine. And I have been."

"I didn't even ask if you were comfortable around it."

"Oh, it doesn't bother me when people have a beer or glass of wine or a cocktail. I don't like being around people who've had one too many, but I don't mind those who handle it responsibly. What?" He turned to her surprised face.

"I'm just... I'm trying to reconcile the image I have of you in high school to what I know now. I never once saw you drink back then, but it was so easy for me to believe what people said. Was I always that foolish to just accept what I'd been told and not pay attention?"

"You were in high school, Billy Lou. Your world consisted of cheer, Jerry, and school. Deep observations weren't exactly a priority. Cut yourself some slack."

"True. I guess you're right. Well, for what it's worth, I'm sorry I believed the rumors about you."

"Most people did. But thanks." He smiled at her as

he exited towards Piney. When they reached the turn towards her house, they both sighed in contentment. He pulled to a stop in her driveway, and they sat a moment.

"What is that?" Billy Lou asked. "Do you hear it?"

Charlie opened his door and music carried to them. "Sounds like it's in your backyard."

Curious, Billy Lou unbuckled her seat belt. "Come on. I think I'm having a party." She tugged his hand around the side of her house and threaded her fingers through his as they walked towards her outdoor entertainment area. The large pergola lit with stringing lights, a small fire in a rock fireplace, and the most heavenly smell of pizza welcomed them. "What is all this?" Billy Lou asked.

Reesa beamed, her eyes flashing briefly to their joined hands. "Welcome back. We're enjoying our night out. I hope you don't mind that we took over your house."

"Why are you four not at the reunion?" Her eyes flashed to Theodore, then Jason, and then to Jamie.

"It wasn't very fun," Jamie replied, her face annoyed at whatever transpired over the course of the night. "So, we decided to make our own."

"Got some more in there?" Charlie pointed to a pizza box and Reesa nodded.

"Still hot."

Charlie began to step forward, but Billy Lou failed to relinquish his hand and held him back. When she realized her hold on him, she let go. "Come on, Billy, have a slice. It's been hours since we ate."

She looked down at her dress and at the others still wearing their formal wear as well. "You know what? Pizza sounds good." She nudged Jason's feet off their resting spot of a free chair and sat as Charlie dished two slices of pizza on paper plates and handed one to her.

"So how was y'all's evening?" Theodore asked.

"Wonderful," Billy Lou replied. "It was beautifully done, as always."

"Were you about to turn into a pumpkin, Mr. Charlie?"

"No, he did wonderful. A good sport the entire evening," Billy Lou reported. "I was pleasantly surprised."

Charlie looked at her teasing gaze and winked. "I wasn't about to call it quits early when I had the honor of being with the prettiest girl there."

Jamie fanned herself at the open flirtation and grinned at her friends as Billy Lou and Charlie stared at one another a moment longer.

"Is Clare here?" Billy Lou asked.

"She is. She was watching a movie a while ago, but last Theo went inside, she'd fallen asleep on the couch," Reesa explained. "Teddy went home once we all showed up."

Charlie eased into a free chair next to Theo and on the other side of Billy Lou and silently ate his pizza.

"Well, y'all are more than welcome to hang out as long as you wish, but I think I'm going to call it an evening." Billy Lou dabbed her lips with her napkin. "These high heels are about to do me in."

Charlie finished his own slice of pizza and shook Theo's hand before offering it to Billy Lou to help her rise to her feet. She wobbled on her heels, her ankles officially done with the assault. Charlie reached under and swooped her off her feet. Billy Lou gasped at the motion and looked flabbergasted. "Charlie Edwards, put me down."

"I got you, Billy." He nodded his farewell to the younger adults and began walking back up the hill towards the house.

"I can walk." Billy Lou, already acquiescing to her new mode of transportation draped her arm around his neck.

"I know, but your feet are hurtin'. I can carry you. You don't weigh much more than a penny."

She chuckled at that, and he felt her head gently rest against his shoulder as she held on. He walked around the side of the house to the front door and gently set her to her feet. "Well, that was lovely." Billy Lou smiled up at him. "Don't think I've been carried in ages."

"My pleasure." He was barely winded, for which he was grateful.

She opened the front door a crack and then hesitated. "Thank you for coming with me tonight, Charlie. I enjoyed it."

"Me too, Billy. Despite having to wear a suit."

Grinning, she brushed invisible lint from his shoulders. "Yes, well, I almost hate to say goodnight to ya. I've enjoyed the look of you in such a fine suit."

His brow lifted at that announcement, and he took a step closer to her. He grabbed one of her hands off his shoulder and held it in both of his. He lifted her hand to his lips. "I don't think I'll ever forget the way you look tonight, Billy." He kissed her knuckles. "Thank you for the honor of escorting you tonight." He released his hold and took a step off the porch towards Theo's truck. "I'm sure he can find a ride home," Charlie announced. He turned to smile at her, but she'd silently followed him, and he halted his steps in complete surprise. "What are y—" His words were stopped by Billy Lou's arms flying around his shoulders. Her lips found his in a rush of warmth and excitement and her hands slid from his shoulders to his face as she tugged him closer to her. He slipped a hand gently around her waist and pressed her against him. He deepened the kiss, not even certain when he'd last kissed a woman in such a way, but Billy Lou responded, and his heart began to thaw in slow satisfying drips at her affection. She tugged her head away from his, their erratic breath mingling in the air around them.

"Good night," Billy Lou whispered, her eyes glistening with the night sky as she looked at him. He wasn't sure what had inspired such a move on her part, but he was certain he'd wake up in the morning to find it only a dream.

"Night, Billy." He squeezed her hand one last time and slid into Theo's truck. Their eyes held a moment, and he couldn't help the smile that burst forth at what had just happened between them. And to his surprise, Billy Lou smiled back at him. He gave a small, shy wave and pulled away from the house.

Chapter Ten

Late nights were no longer in her routine. Each evening she'd make supper and eat by six-thirty. She'd have her kitchen cleaned up by seven. Then she'd shower, change into her pajamas, make a cup of hot herbal tea and find her comfy spot in the living room. She'd turn the television on to whatever suited her fancy, pick up her cross stitch she'd been working on for Clare, and work until her eyes or hands grew tired and her teacup was empty. That was usually by nine. Then she'd turn off the television, take her empty cup to the dishwasher, and head to bed. The routine didn't change other than what she decided to do to keep her hands busy. When she wasn't cross stitching, she'd look over her weekly planner and fill her days with projects or map out flower garden ideas. She kept busy until she eventually drifted off to sleep. The evenings were quiet, and since Jerry's passing, somewhat lonely. She missed his presence. His booming voice and laugh. His positive energy that bounced around the house. But he was gone. Some days she could still sense that energy, as if he'd left some behind to get her through the hard years of his absence. Billy Lou remembered the day of cleaning out his dresser drawers and his closet. She'd kept a few things, of course, but the act of removing articles of clothing she remembered him wearing, making memories in, had kept her in the house for weeks. Mounds of clothes piled on the bed, and she slept in the midst of them, surrounded by his scent, until she had to come to terms with the fact he wasn't coming back. She wouldn't hear him whistling outside while he trimmed the roses. She wouldn't hear his stereo in the garage when he was polishing the Corvette. And she wouldn't smell the heavenly smell of his coffee in the mornings as she awoke. Those were memories now. Now, she drove into town and fetched a coffee at Java Jamie's. That was her 'fresh start' to her mornings, her new routine, though she was later this morning than normal because she'd had such a late night at the gala with Charlie. Her face warmed at the thought of kissing him the night before. She still couldn't believe she'd done it. And she was even more surprised, looking back on it this morning in relation to reminiscing about Jerry, that she wasn't upset with herself. The usual feelings of disloyalty and guilt were lighter than before, not as prevalent as they had been. And she wondered if this new feeling of release was a touch of her grief moving on without her, or if it buried itself away deeper into her heart only to pop out on another rainy day later on down the road. Dread creeped in at the thought of that. She didn't want that. She was tired of those days. She was tired of feeling joyful and hopeful one moment and then swallowed up by loss the next. Feeling lighter this morning was a relief, wasn't it?

She opened the door to Java Jamie's, the bell jingling its familiar happy tune, and her face bloomed into a warm smile at the sight of her two favorite women. Reesa sat on one of the couches, her hands vigorously working on a crochet project, the multitude of vibrant colors a direct reflection of the woman's personality. Jamie stood behind the counter, her usual bouncy red hair tied up into a tight bun as she bent over to pipe cream into popovers. Her head raised and she stood. "Well, hello gorgeous!"

"Morning, girls." Billy Lou looked them both over. "Well, you two don't look like you were up until all hours of the night. What time did you all call it quits?"

"Two, I think." Reesa looked to Jamie in agreement.

"Oh my word." Billy Lou shook her head. "I don't know how you girls are up and walking around."

"You just missed Mr. Charlie," Jamie announced,

and Billy Lou's head snapped back to face her.

"Oh?"

"Yep. Came and got his morning brew from yours truly." Jamie fluffed a hand over her bun.

"Is he as tired as I am?" Billy Lou asked on a chuckle.

"Didn't seem to be. He seemed upset about something, though, didn't he, Reesa?"

"Yeah, he wasn't his usual self."

"Oh?" Billy Lou asked again.

"Yeah, I asked him if something was botherin' him. He brushed it off with that charm of his, but I could tell something was eating at him." Jamie looked up as the bell above the door signalled a new customer. Her face fell slightly as Jason Wright walked in with another beautiful woman.

"Morning, Jamie," he greeted. "Look who I bumped into." He pointed to the woman beside him who already had stars in her eyes when he smiled at her. "Leslie Chapin from the reunion last night."

"Fun." Jamie's face held a stiff, but polite smile as she asked for their order.

Billy Lou quietly slipped away and found a seat near Reesa. Reesa looked up over her crochet hook and hot pink yarn. "You're hiding something," she said, her eyes holding Billy Lou's a moment before she went back to her stitches. She paused briefly to count and then her fingers went about their familiar dance.

"I'm not hiding a thing." Billy Lou set her purse by her feet and nodded over her shoulder towards the counter. "How'd it go with those two last night?"

"They seemed to have fun. Jason was great. Jamie is always great."

"And then he walks in with Leslie Chapin." Billy Lou's harsh whisper and look of distaste told Reesa all she needed to know about Leslie. "That girl was after Jason and Theodore in high school. She wasn't... subtle," Billy Lou added.

"Interesting. I don't even remember her from the reunion, but we only stayed an hour or so. Jason was all about hanging with all of us last night, and he and Jamie seemed to hit it off. I guess he was just being..."

"Jason." Billy Lou shook her head in disappointment and hated that Jamie was having to feel the sting of disappointed hopes. "Bless her heart. I like Jason, but sometimes I just want to hit him upside the head."

Reesa giggled under her breath. "I often think of doing that to Theo."

"He's had plenty in his life, so when he needs another, you do what you need to do, honey."

Laughing, Reesa eyed Billy Lou over her project.

"You sure you're okay?"

"I'm fine. I had a lovely evening last night, and have had a laid back morning. I'm concerned about Charlie, that's all. He was upset, you said?"

"Maybe not upset, just not his usual social self. I got the feeling that something was weighing on his mind. I didn't pry, though you know that's exactly what I wanted to do. I figured something happened between the two of you last night and maybe he was mulling it over."

Billy Lou choked on her sip of coffee. "Why on earth would you think something happened?" She felt her cheeks grow hot, and she felt even more nervous when Reesa's eyes lit up in acknowledgement.

"Ah... so something *did* happen. Billy Lou you have to tell me." Reesa squealed and bounced in her seat. "Oh my goodness, Jamie has to be in on this conversation. Don't say anything yet."

"Reesa, honey,"

"No, no, no. Don't honey me." She pointed at Billy Lou until the latter felt her resolve slip a touch and Reesa, giddy, waved at Jamie. "You better hurry up!" she yelled.

Jamie looked at the two of them and her usual energetic bounce returned. She hurriedly accepted payment from Jason. "Sorry, coffee shop's closed. Come again." She shooed them to the door and Jason looked at her like she'd lost her mind.

"Jamie, what has gotten into you?" He kept walking towards the door, his boots hesitant and tripping with each step, and a stunned Leslie following him as Jamie nudged him in the back.

"Love you to death, Jason, but there's important matters that need to be discussed. Have a good day. Good to see you, Leslie. Bye!" she yelled after them as she all but shoved them out the door and flipped the lock. She turned her 'Open' sign to 'Closed' and hurried towards the sofa with Reesa. "Okay, spill."

"Something happened between Billy Lou and Charlie last night," Reesa announced. "but she's holding out on me."

Jamie gasped and then eased into a seated position next to Reesa, but on the edge of the sofa as if she were ready to spring at any moment. "Billy Lou!" She squealed and then lightly tapped Billy Lou's knee in excitement. "What happened?"

"You girls." Billy Lou shook her head on a chuckle. "We had a nice evening together. Charlie is a nice man, and it was nice to get to know the Charlie of today rather than the Charlie I remembered from high school."

"What's the difference?" Jamie asked curiously.

"Well, come to find out, my perception of him in high school wasn't totally accurate."

The two women listened as Billy Lou shared small tidbits, but nothing she felt would betray Charlie's trust. "And he was a gentleman and kind the entire night."

"And was there any... chemistry?" Reesa asked, her polite attempt at containing her over excitement was evident and Billy Lou appreciated her efforts.

Sighing, Billy Lou set her coffee aside. "Girls—," She looked at her hands a moment.

Jamie reached across and placed her hand on Billy Lou's. "You don't have to tell us anything, Billy Lou. We love you and respect you, and we are just happy if you're happy. And if you're not happy, then we'll kick some Charlie butt."

Billy Lou chuckled and squeezed her hand in thanks. "You two have been such blessings to me. I adore the both of you. Despite our age difference, I consider you the best of friends."

"Likewise," Reesa said. "Slash mom substitute sometimes."

Billy Lou placed a hand on her heart. "And I love that too. And Charlie... well, he's been a surprise, hasn't he?"

Reesa compassionately smiled.

"I have much to sort out in regards to Charlie Edwards. He's a good man. And he... well... he makes me feel special."

"You are," Jamie concurred.

Smiling in thanks, Billy Lou's eyes grew glassy.

"Yes, well, I had a lovely husband who made me feel that way every day for decades. It's hard to accept that he's gone and at the same time embrace the possibility of something new without feeling guilty or, quite frankly, scared."

The two younger women listened with empathy and kindness. Reesa had set aside her crochet and was fully focused upon Billy Lou's words.

"Did you and Charlie talk about a future?"

"No." Billy Lou shook her head. "I imagine that's what has him equally vexed. There was a shift for us both last night. I'm not sure if he would even want a future with me. This is just me reading too much into everything. I just know a conversation will be happening soon. And for both of us, I hope that conversation ends with us remaining friends, no matter what. I'll admit, it was me who changed the playing field. And I don't even know if the thought had crossed his mind up to that point."

"Oh, it has," Jamie assured her. "You've just been blind. He's had eyes for you, Billy Lou, from the beginning."

"Well, whether he does or not, that's for him to sort out, and for us to discuss. I have to make sure my heart is in the right place, too. I can't keep bouncing between my past and my present and comparing the two. My present and my future are different. When Jerry passed away, that changed my course and my plans. So, now I have to sort out what all that looks like for me personally, with or without Charlie factored in. I never considered someone else in my future equation for life. Not until last night. And... I'm trying to sort out how I feel in regard to that possibility."

Reesa jumped to her feet. "Theo's at the door."

"We'll talk more of this later." Billy Lou leaned back in her chair and reached for her coffee again.

"After you talk to Charlie," Jamie whispered. "Here if you need me, Ms. Billy Lou."

"I know, sweetie, thank you."

Jamie hopped to her feet. "T.J., can't I take a break from you? I just needed five minutes of girl time. Geez!"

Billy Lou chuckled at Jamie's antagonistic approach to her grandson as he surveyed each face to make sure nothing was wrong in the midst of their abnormal behavior. His eyes landed on hers and she offered a welcoming smile and a nod. No one else needed to know of her inward battle, especially Theodore. But the one person she did want to see and talk to was Charlie Edwards.

^

He'd attempted to work on the house. He'd reframed the sagging porch and replaced rotted support beams. Jason had swung by to check his work for him and approved it, so he laid a new porch. It was done. He sat on the freshly sanded front steps and sipped at his now cold coffee and enjoyed watching the birds fly overhead and the wind whistling through the pines. The breeze held a light scent of sap that took him back to watching his momma hang clothes on the line and he and his brothers rough housin' in the front yard over a worn-out football. He remembered sitting on the porch and having bowls of homemade ice cream with fresh peaches or strawberries, his momma's special treat for them after they'd finish a hard day of tilling a new garden bed for her. He could see the scene before him: the smell of the grass on his clothes, the scent of the fresh linens on the line, and her sweet perfume; memories long faded, but rejuvenated alongside the tired porch. Replacing the old with the new. How many people would sit on this porch in the future? How many babies would learn to walk along the beams? How many heartfelt chats would take place on the very steps he sat on? Or first kisses by the door? His mind wandered to Billy Lou's kiss from the night before. He hadn't been rocked by a woman's kiss in a long time. He actually couldn't even remember the last time. His heart had 'bout jumped out of his chest in the moment. And thinking about it now had his pulse kicking up a slight notch once more.

What had happened between them last night? He felt a shift, that was for sure, but what kind? And was she caught up in the moment, or did she genuinely have feelings for him? It was odd thinking of such a thing, especially at his age. He wasn't a young buck anymore. He was seasoned, weathered, old, and usually tired. He harrumphed at his own distaste of that, but he felt his body slowing down year by year. It was part of the aging process. And he'd aged just like the rest of the people in the world. No one was immune. But to consider a new relationship at his age seemed almost daunting. Did he like Billy Lou? Of course. Did he find her beautiful? Definitely. Did he want to marry someone and settle down this late in life? He wasn't even considering it. The whole idea of factoring someone into his life in such a way at this stage in his life sounded exhausting. And looking around at the work before him on the house and the two trucks he planned to restore before his days were done, he just didn't see how he could factor in anything else, especially something of such magnitude.

Young Teddy Graham poked his head out of his shed, wiping his hands on a grease towel. The teenager had been loyal and disciplined in his offer to work wherever Charlie put him. Since finding out about Clare's potential new ride, Teddy had been elbow deep in grease, just like Charlie knew he'd be. He currently had him dismantling the truck. With guidance, he'd been focused upon cleaning those parts for the last two hours. "Mr. Charlie, I think I'm at a stopping point for now. I was going to go grab some lunch if you don't mind."

"Not at all. You've been busy."

Teddy continued to walk towards him and admired the porch. "You have too. This looks awesome." He stepped on the bottom step and sat beside Charlie. "Man, I don't know how you do all this stuff. This looks like something Mr. Wright would do."

Charlie grinned and patted the young man on his back. "You learn a lot of different skills in life when you've lived as long as I have, son."

"I feel like I'm just starting." Teddy shook his head at his stained hands. "I appreciate you letting me help on the trucks. I don't know much about vehicles other than what Theo's taught me the last year or so. I'm doing my best to learn more, but I don't have much of a chance to test my knowledge. Those trucks in there are sure testing me."

Chuckling, Charlie nodded. "And this is just the beginning. I hope you'll stick one out from start to finish. By then, you'll be an expert."

Baffled, Teddy glanced towards the shed. "I doubt that, but I will at least know the basics."

"Son, taking apart a truck is difficult in itself. Putting it back together is hard. Then actually making it run is another game. If you're able to accomplish all three, then you've got it made."

"How many cars you had?"

"About a hundred, give or take a few."

Teddy's eyes widened. "A *hundred*?"

"I didn't restore that many though," Charlie clarified. "Sometimes I'd buy a cheap fixer upper and use it for parts. Sometimes I'd just buy and trade or buy and resell it at a different price point. And then some I restored."

"What was your favorite?"

Charlie hissed as if the question stung. "I don't know if that question has an answer. There's too many. Though I was rather attached to a 1934 Ford convertible. Man, it was a piece of work. Probably the best work I've ever done. And they're rare, so it added a touch of whimsy to the project."

"Wow. What else have you restored?"

"Oh, let's see... a 1937 Chevy Coup. Real pretty black one, cream interior that was so smooth it'd make you cry."

Teddy grinned.

"A 1939 Ford two-door sedan called the Grey Ghost." Charlie winked at him. "It was slick as could be. Actually won a few awards at the Queen Wilhelmena Rod Run over in Mena."

"Do you still have it?"

"Oh, no. I sold it about fifteen years ago or so. It sure was pretty, though."

"Sounds like it." Teddy sat quietly a moment. "Think we could go to one of those shows sometime? Mena isn't too far."

Touched and excited about the prospect of sharing his love of street rods with the younger generation, Charlie nodded emphatically. "Sure! Why not? We'll even rope Clare into coming too. She needs to see the possibilities of that truck of hers."

"Awesome." Teddy stood to his feet. "Well, I'm going to go get something to eat. Want me to bring you something back?"

"That's alright. I think I've got a sandwich in the cooler. And take your time, Teddy. No rush on that pickup."

"Yes sir. Thank you, sir." His lanky legs climbed into his own pickup and shut the door. As he was headed out the drive, he slowed and stopped to talk to an oncoming Billy Lou, whose SUV glistened in the afternoon sun.

Charlie's quick intake of breath had him dreading the conversation that was about to follow. He wondered if he should be working when she pulled up in order to avoid as much forced eye contact as a conversation required or if he should stay seated where he was. His tiredness kept him where he sat, and he glanced up when he heard her car door close. She stood there a moment and walked towards the house, pausing to cross her arms over her chest as she surveyed his latest project.

"Well, I'd say that porch is quite spiffy."

"You think so?" He patted the wooden beam beneath him. "This step might have a little sag to it after my lengthy break of sitting on it."

Billy Lou smirked as she walked closer to the house and eased onto the step beside him. She looked out over the yard and the property and inhaled a deep breath of piney woods as well. "A nice spot."

"I thought so too." Charlie looked out over the landscape as well. "I'm growing more and more fond of it."

"It's lunch time," Billy Lou commented.

"Yep. That's where Teddy is headed."

"And you've already built a porch for the day."

"Yep. And I'm exhausted."

They both chuckled at his remark.

"How about I steal you away for lunch?"

"Oh?" He looked at her a moment, but her eyes were still fixated on the landscape around them.

"Where to?"

"My house." Billy Lou stood. "I made chicken salad sandwiches, a Caesar salad, and sweet tea."

"Now that sounds inviting. I'm pretty filthy."

"I can see that." She finally looked at him and eased to his own two feet. "But you'll do."

His lips quirked at that as he followed her towards her car. "Might get mud in your car."

"No, you won't," she quipped, and hopped behind the wheel.

When he slid in, he realized she'd put a sheet of parchment paper on the floor mat just for him. He laughed and her eyes danced in amusement. "You're good."

"I know." She pulled away and drove the short distance to her house. "I was going to wrap everything up and just bring a picnic, but it's hard to do that with salad. I wanted it to stay crisp." She pulled into her garage and parked the car. Leading the way into the house and through a small mudroom, they entered her kitchen. She pointed to the sink and he obediently walked over and began washing his hands. "I appreciate the lunch."

"We can eat on the patio." She pointed out the window and he could see a table already set for two. She withdrew her dishes from the refrigerator and carried them outside, the warm, light breeze inviting as he joined her. He sat, watching her go through the motions of removing covers and lids, and then handed him a glass of tea. "This little table has become one of my favorite places to eat and sit when the weather's pretty."

"It's nice." Charlie waited for her hands to settle.

Her eyes finally met his a brief moment before glancing back to the food. She said a quick grace and then handed him the bowl of salad. "I wanted to talk with you." He looked up at her as she prepared a croissant with chicken salad. Her hands stayed busy as she spoke. "Thank you for attending the gala with me last night. Again, it was a lovely evening and I appreciate you going with me."

He didn't say anything in response and continued fixing his plate full of the delicious food. His first bite told him she'd made her dressing from scratch and the flavor was so fantastic he couldn't help the sound that slipped from his mouth. She eyed him curiously and he pointed his fork at his plate until he'd swallowed. "That might be the best salad dressing I've ever tasted, Billy. Wow." He paused a moment to take a sip of tea and then waved his hand for her to continue. "Sorry to interrupt. Keep talking."

Her eyes narrowed slightly but her lips curved into a pleased expression. "Anyway," she continued. "I wanted to also say… well, I'm not sorry."

Confused, he looked at her. "For what?"

"I'm not sorry I kissed you last night," she stated, her words slightly breaking at the end, betraying nerves he didn't believe existed in Billy Lou.

"Oh." He gently set his fork down next to his plate.

"Now, before you get all quiet on me, I'm going to say what I have to say, and then you can just do what you want with it. Alright?"

"Fair enough," Charlie agreed, and nodded for her to continue.

"I'm not sorry I kissed you because, quite frankly, it was nice." His lips curled up at the corners and she pointed at him with a stern finger. "Don't get cocky," she warned before continuing. "I hadn't realized I'd even wanted to kiss you until I had. It surprised me, as I'm sure it surprised you. Now, I've been stewin' about it, thinking it over, dealing with it, whatever you want to call it, and I've realized that... well, I think I kind of like you, Charlie."

His brows lifted in surprise.

"I know. I'm shocked as well. I still feel torn about the idea, but it's the conclusion I've come to, and I'm still sortin' out the details, but I like you. That being said, I think we should discuss it, because I don't want things to be awkward between us should you feel differently." She waved her hand for him to feel free to talk. He was speechless. He never in a million years considered this to be the direction this particular conversation would go. Billy Lou Waldrup liked him. "I don't quite know what to say, Billy."

"I know, I've sort of thrown a wrench in everything with my announcement, but to be fair, you've done the very same just by being here. So, man up, Charlie Edwards, because I have, and I'm dealing with this new... *thing*." She leaned back in her chair and studied him.

"Well... I reckon I feel... about the same as you, I guess."

"You guess?"

"I guess."

She nodded in understanding.

"But I'm also not sure quite how I feel about it all."

"It all, being what?" Billy Lou asked.

"You know, the details. Like, what are we? Do we date? What's that look like at our age? Is it tiring? Is it fun? Where do we go? What do we do?" He waved his hand as if the questions went on and on. "And it... overwhelms me."

"Good." Relief flooded out of her, and she reached for his hand. "It overwhelms me too."

He relaxed as he turned his hand over and held hers palm to palm. "I do like you, Billy. And I do care for you. I just don't know what it is you want in life now or what I'm even able to give at this point. You had a great marriage with Jerry. You built a life together. I've never had that. I built my life on my own. I've always been on my own. I don't know where to even start factoring in another person in my life."

Billy Lou scooted her seat closer and draped her arm over the back of his chair. "Well, for starters, you tell me how beautiful I am every day, even though I grow older by the minute."

He turned to face her and he nodded. "That won't be hard to do because you're still the prettiest girl in Piney."

She narrowed her eyes.

"I meant in the entire state of Arkansas."

One brow lifted.

"The world," he corrected, and she grinned.

"And then," she went on, leaning closer to him. "every now and then, I might require a little TLC."

"And what's that entail?" Charlie asked.

"Well, a walk together, a meal on the patio, a hug, or maybe a kiss."

"Hmmm..." Charlie rubbed a hand over his chin. "That doesn't sound like too bad of a gig."

"No?" she asked with a quirk of her brow.

"What else is there?"

"Well, you don't have to call me sweetie or anything like that. I'm not really into pet names."

"But you call everyone honey and sweetie," he pointed out.

"Yes, but that doesn't mean I like to be called that."

"Alright, so what do I call you?"

She leaned closer to him. "Billy."

"But you hate when I call you Billy." He reached up

and tucked a strand of her white hair behind her ear, his finger lightly curving and brushing down her cheek.

"It's growing on me."

Chapter Eleven

Billy Lou sat at her small dinette table, leaning over Clare's stitching ring. "Yep, yep... just right through like that. You just follow that pattern of blue squares."

"Ouch." Clare hissed and pulled her finger to her lips.

"Yep, gotta watch that needle, honey." She swiftly threaded her own needle and began her work on another tea towel for her young friend. "You'll get the hang of it."

Clare sighed as she tediously poked her needle through the fabric and gently tugged. "There. Two stitches complete."

"See, already accomplished."

Clare's feet bounced with excess energy as she looked longingly out the window at Theo, Charlie, and her mother sitting on the patio. "How long until the cookies are done?"

Billy Lou turned her head to peek at the timer on the counter. "Three more minutes."

Clare sighed again. "What do you think they're talking about?"

"Does it matter?" Billy Lou asked.

"I don't know. Aren't you curious?"

"Not really. I imagine they'll tell us when we go out there."

"Oh, look. Theo and Charlie are walkin' down towards the pond."

Billy Lou smirked at her impatience. "Go on." Billy Lou gestured towards the door. "Go on."

"Really?" Clare's hopeful tone had her laughing.

"Yes. Go be nosy."

Clare set her cross-stitch pattern on the table and hopped to her feet. "I'll be back in a couple of minutes to check the cookies!" she called over her shoulder as she bolted out the door, past her mother, and after the two men.

Reesa popped her head inside the door. "Everything okay in here?"

"Oh yes, Clare didn't want to be left out."

Reesa rolled her eyes and stepped into the house. Without asking, she walked over to the oven and checked the cookies. "Almost done." She then spotted the timer. "Ah." She walked over and picked up Clare's abandoned project. "Not bad so far."

"She'll get there if she can master a bit more patience with it."

Reesa set it aside. "How are you doing, Billy Lou?"

"I'm fine." Billy Lou smiled as she set aside her own project. "Why do you ask?"

"You just seem... different lately."

"Do I?"

"Yes." Reesa eyed her carefully. "Anything *new* happening in your life lately?"

Billy Lou rose to her feet and walked to the oven and removed the pan of butterscotch cookies. "He told you and Theo, didn't he?"

Reesa squealed and did a happy dance before throwing her arms around Billy Lou's shoulders. Laughing, Billy Lou patted Reesa's back in response. "I'm happy for you."

"Really? I could hardly tell."

Reesa gave her one last big squeeze before releasing her and stealing a hot cookie off the pan and bouncing it back and forth between her hands. "So, how'd this all come about? I thought you were dead set against a new relationship."

"I honestly don't have an answer for you, Reesa. It just sort of evolved. Charlie's a good man. I also had to let go of some of my past opinions of him as I learned more about him. I had to come to terms with my own grief over Jerry." She paused. "Now, I know that will never fully go away, but my heart is a little less sad all the time, and I'm finding moments of happiness with Charlie that are fresh and new, and that's nothing to feel guilty about. That's the hard part some days, but he's willing to be patient with me there, as I'm willing to be patient with his utter lack of knowledge in regard to serious relationships. We both have some growing to do together. That's kind of nice to be as old as we are and realize we still have some room for growth in our lives. And we'd like to help each other with that."

"I think that's wonderful." Reesa beamed. "So... I guess that means he's staying in Piney?"

Billy Lou nodded. "I believe he is, if all things go well."

"Theo knew, didn't he?"

"Yes. Charlie wanted to make sure Theodore was alright with the change in our friendship before openly pursuing me, so to speak, out of respect for his relationship with Jerry."

"Why didn't he tell me?" Reesa pondered and then waved it away. "Doesn't matter. Super exciting.

Does Jamie know?"

"Honey, it's been three days. I don't think the entire county knows yet."

"Well, you'll have to tell her. She's going to be so excited. And upset."

"Upset? Why?"

"Well, in an odd way, the two of you are going to break her heart. One: no more hot dates to galas with you, and two: Charlie's off the market."

Billy Lou hooted in laughter.

"The two hottest people in Piney are out of the game now."

"You two girls." Billy Lou shook her head. "You crack me up. Somethin' tells me Jamie will be just fine. That girl has too much sunshine for the right man not to notice soon."

Clare threw open the back door, winded from sprinting up the hill from the pond. "Cookies?" she panted.

"Already out of the oven."

She bent over to take a deep breath and then stood. "Okay, good. I forgot."

Billy Lou waved her back out the door and they both watched her sprint back towards the men.

"I'm thankful she has them to spend time with." Reesa watched as her daughter, at a full sprint, hopped on her last step and threw herself onto an unsuspecting Theo's back as he stood by Charlie. Her force and weight caught him off guard and he stumbled forward a step before righting himself. "He's such a good sport." Reesa chuckled at her daughter's antics and watched as Clare rested her chin on Theo's shoulder, as her boyfriend acquiesced to being a mode of transportation piggy-back style for Clare. Charlie bent down and plucked a flower and handed it to Clare, the teen soaking up all the attention. "She's going to be so spoiled by the time she graduates high school."

"It's good for her." Billy Lou draped her arm around Reesa's shoulders. "Come on, we can't let her steal all the attention. We must keep her humble, after all."

"You're exactly right." Reesa opened the door and then turned back, bumping into Billy Lou. "Wait, we need cookies. We'll beat her at her own game."

Laughing, the two women grabbed napkins with multiple cookies to share before walking outside. Reesa wafted the scent in the air as she grew close, and both men's eyes lit up at the sight of the treat. "Clare, leave Theo alone," Reesa warned, handing her boyfriend a warm cookie.

Charlie accepted the cookie from Billy Lou and took a bite. His brows lifted and he looked at her in wonder. "Wow. Is this part of the plan too? Fresh baked cookies to look forward to?"

She linked her arm with his and rested her head

on his shoulder. One thing she had already noticed with Charlie was that even a small gesture of a cookie surprised him. He wasn't used to receiving such goodies. So, naturally, Billy Lou had baked the last three days. Banana bread, muffins, cookies. She wanted him to know how much she enjoyed cooking, but also that she liked doing it for him. So far, he'd yet to turn down anything she'd made. "I'll add them to the list."

He looked down and into her eyes. "I'm liking the list we're putting together."

"Me too." She smiled up at him. "Now, are you two men going to stare at that water, or are you going to catch us some supper?" Billy Lou clapped her hands and walked over to the abandoned fishing poles, and handed one to both Theo and Charlie. "Get after it, boys. I want some fried catfish." She winked at Charlie as she linked arms with Reesa and Clare. "And you boys better hurry, because the day is moving fast."

"Well, you've got some nerve showing up here without coffee." Billy Lou fisted her hands on her hips as she looked at a cheerful Jamie in a pair of bright blue overalls with her red curls tied up in a silk bandana.

"I came to work. I didn't even walk into the shop this morning," Jamie admitted, her eyes studying how much work had been done to Charlie's house since she'd last laid eyes on it. "Man, it looks like a completely different house, doesn't it?"

"He's been working hard," Billy Lou complimented.

"I think everyone has." Jamie pointed to a filthy Teddy Graham as he lifted another panel of siding to nail in place. His face was streaked with dirt and sweat, and Billy Lou beamed proudly. "He has been a blessing to Charlie, that's for certain."

"Where is Charlie?" Jamie asked.

"He's inside with Jason looking at the finished project of the giant hole in the floor."

"Ah, the 'spare oom', hm?"

Billy Lou waved her onward and Jamie entered the house. "Well, hey there, handsome," she called.

Jason turned with a brilliant white smile, but her eyes didn't even glance at the man. Her eyes were on Charlie, and he grinned at the younger man's slight disappointment. "Hey, gorgeous. I was hoping you'd come see me."

"Like you could keep me away." Jamie giggled and then playfully punched Jason on the shoulder in greeting. "Nice work, handyman."

He laughed and nodded his thanks.

"I disappointed your number one woman out there because I didn't bring coffee with me." Jamie feigned a grimace and Charlie patted her on the shoulder.

"Some days, there's just no pleasin' Billy Lou. Today is one of those days."

"I hardly think asking for more butter on my biscuit at breakfast qualifies as me being hard to please." Billy Lou's voice drifted down the hallway and Charlie's eyes widened at being overheard.

"I don't know how she does that sometimes. So, are you my extra help today?" he asked Jamie.

She nodded. "Reesa was launching a pattern this morning and said she'd be over in a few, Clare is coming with Theo after work,and I closed the shop today because I wanted a break and some fresh air."

"Well, I can't guarantee this being much of a break, but I've got a project for you." Charlie motioned for her to follow him, and she did so with enthusiasm.

"Wow, it's really coming around. I love that first bedroom's wall color."

"I'm glad you like it, because I was hoping you'd paint the living room walls that color as well."

"Ooooooh." Jamie clapped her hands together. "You got it."

"You don't mind painting?"

"Not at all." Jamie pulled a small speaker out of her pocket and her phone. "As long as you don't mind me jammin' while I do it."

Charlie helped Jamie set up shop in the

living room and she was already dancing and jiving while doing an impeccable job of covering the wall with new paint.

Reesa walked inside with two large cans of floor polish. "I'm ready to transform this old wood and make it beautiful. I hope this is what you meant when you said floor polish. I did ask the workers at the store if this would work on wood floors, and they assured me it would."

"That's exactly what it is. I thought you were working?"

"I was. I'm done. And good on this stuff... because it is heavy." She carried it to the back bedroom. "I'll start back here and work my way to the front. Oh! Hi, Jason."

He left them all to their jobs and stepped outside. Billy Lou sat on the porch flipping through a home and garden magazine. "What are you up to?"

"I'm piecing together an idea on how to decorate the interior."

"Why would I need to decorate the inside?"

"Well, don't you plan on living here?"

Charlie shook his head, and he watched as fear slipped behind her gaze. "I plan to stay in Piney, Billy, just not here at this house."

"Why not?"

Sighing, Charlie looked around. "I just… don't want to. I don't know how to say it other than that. It hasn't felt like home since I was a kid, and it certainly doesn't feel like home to me now."

"But where will you live? And what about the trucks?"

"Oh, I plan to keep them here. I don't plan on selling the place yet, just maybe rent it out for a while."

"Rent houses get eaten up and spit out, Charlie. The work you've done to this place would just be ruined in a matter of months."

"Not if I find the right person."

"And again, where would you live?"

"Oh, Theo said there's some apartments in Piney that aren't too bad."

"Apartment?" Billy Lou shook her head. "We'll have to discuss this some more. I don't like the idea of you living in some apartment."

"Why not?" Baffled, he looked up at her as she paced and he sat.

"Because this house is beautiful."

"And it's not for me," Charlie stated.

"What about poor, Sugar? She needs a yard to run in."

"She'll be fine."

"She needs a house to feel safe."

"She's a dog. I think she'll feel safe with me."

"Well, I'll buy it, then."

"And do what with it, Billy? You have a house twice as beautiful as this one."

"I'll give it to Theodore."

"And what about his house?"

"He can use it as a hunting cabin."

"In the same town that he lives? He would never use it as such, and you know it. Plus, that place is Theo's and he loves it. This place will make a happy home for someone else."

"Sometimes I wish I could just up and sell everything and be okay with it." Billy Lou admitted. "but I love my home. I've worked hard on it, tended to it, shaped it into the place it is. It's my haven, and I love it. It's just hard for me to understand sometimes when people don't feel the same way about their own homes. I understand why you don't want to live here, Charlie. I just... hate to see you cut ties with it."

He reached for her hand, and she helped him to his feet. He tugged her into his arms and hugged her tight. He liked the feel of Billy in his arms and still hadn't quite grown used to it. "I'm okay, Billy, I really am."

She nodded that she understood, and he released

her. "Now... let me show you something." He hurried off into his shed and withdrew a square item wrapped in brown paper. "When Theo gets here, I'm going to unveil this." Billy Lou reached for it and he tugged it just out of reach of her fingertips. "No peeking. You have to wait like everybody else."

"Oh, hog wash. I'm your..." She paused, not quite sure what to add to the end of the sentence and he laughed.

"Go on, say it," he encouraged her with a wide grin. "You're my girl." He tugged her to him and planted a firm kiss to her lips before leaning back just enough to give her a sly wink.

Epilogue

Theo bumped against her shoulder as he shuffled closer to her and made room for Clare and Reesa to squeeze in next to him as they all stood in the living room of Charlie's house. Jason stood to the right, Jamie to the left, Billy Lou and her gang in the middle, and Teddy sort of lingering between them and Jamie. Charlie stood before them in front of the stone fireplace, holding the brown package. The fireplace, thanks to Billy Lou's incessant scrubbing, looked bright and cheerful, the wood mantle freshly sanded, stained, and sealed to a gleam. The entire house looked more put together than any of them believed it could. Charlie smiled proudly as he looked from person to person.

"I can't thank you all enough for what you have

helped me accomplish here. This house... well, there wasn't many good memories here. I'm sure you could tell from the state of the place that it wasn't owned by a particularly happy or healthy person. I suppose my daddy did the best he could considering his condition. Doesn't excuse him for other things, but the house... well, I imagine it was a constant reminder to him of those other failures, mistakes, and losses. It was bound to be reflected here at some point. When I drove up and saw the place after being gone so long, I was angry. Angry at him. Angry at myself." He paused a moment to collect himself. "Just angry at the state it was in. You see, my momma was a wonderful lady. Beautiful, smart, sweet, and funny. The best mom a kid could ask for. When she died, this house lost its light. It was never the same. But today, when I look at it and see it like this..." He waved his hand around the brightly painted room, the clean walls and floors, the repaired doors and door frames, and sighed. "It feels like her place again. Warm. Inviting. Hopeful. I haven't seen it like that since she was here."

He held up his finger to keep everyone's attention. "However, someone else saw it like it used to be." He untied the ribbon on the package and moved the paper. Jamie's painting of his house was fitted in a wooden frame. "Jamie, I'd like this to be a part of the house." He set it in the center of the mantle. "Bringing the past to the present." He reached for Billy Lou's hand, and she stepped towards him and nestled into his side. "Which I've come to find quite lovely about Piney."

Reesa walked forward and draped her arms around the both of them in a group hug, followed by Jamie who excitedly did it on a squeal. She waved everyone else over. "Come on, T.J., get in on this lovin'! You too, Teddy." She pulled the lanky teen into a bone crushing squeeze as he entered the tight circle. Clare tugged Jason over too and Billy Lou soaked in the love of the moment.

"Alright now, we can't breathe." Everyone eased away from the elderly couple and Billy Lou looked up into Charlie's smiling face. The tenderness she saw there made her heart flutter and she embraced that feeling, cherishing it. She'd never thought she would feel that way again, and yet, light as a feather, there it was.

"We should celebrate." Reesa pointed to Jamie.

"Girl, I am *way* ahead of you. I already have pizzas headed to T.J.'s house."

"Why my house?" Theo asked.

"Because I knew it would bug you." Jamie grinned and Jason laughed at the annoyed expression on Theo's face.

"Do they usually team up on you like that?" he asked.

Theo nodded.

"It's one of the many reasons he loves us." Reesa looped her arms around Theo's waist. "Isn't that right, Theo?"

"Don't push it, Mom," Clare warned. "We like him and don't want to scare him off."

"I doubt that would ever happen." Charlie tugged on Clare's ponytail, and she smiled, giving him a quick hug before nudging Teddy out the door and to his truck to reach Theo's cabin first.

Billy Lou and Charlie stood on the porch watching them all head to their vehicles and towards supper, the setting sun shining through the pine trees as it started its final dip in the sky.

This was her family now. Her wonderful grandson and the love of his life, a wonderful young lady she'd get to witness growing into womanhood, and a man she'd long forgotten but now only wished to know more. Times were different for her now. Life was different. But life continued on, and she knew, deep down, Jerry would want that for her too. So, instead of that old familiar feeling of grief swelling in her chest, for the first time in a long time, Billy Lou felt hopeful and truly happy.

Continue the story with...

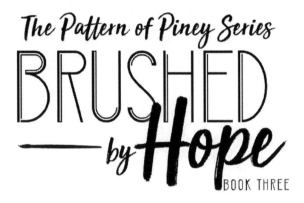

https://www.amazon.com/dp/B0BDYXW43T

INTRODUCING THE FAMILY

THE SIBLINGS O'RIFCAN SERIES   KATHARINE E. HAMILTON

The Complete Siblings O'Rifcan Series Available in Paperback, Ebook, and Audiobook

Claron
https://www.amazon.com/dp/B07FYR44KX

Riley
https://www.amazon.com/dp/B07G2RBD8D

Layla
https://www.amazon.com/dp/B07HJRL67M

Chloe
https://www.amazon.com/dp/B07KB3HG6B

Murphy
https://www.amazon.com/dp/B07N4FCY8V

The Brothers of Hastings Ranch Series Available in Paperback, Ebook, and Audiobook

You can find the entire series here:
https://www.amazon.com/dp/B089LL1JJQ

All titles in The Lighthearted Collection Available in Paperback, Ebook, and Audiobook

Chicago's Best
https://www.amazon.com/dp/B06XH7Y3MF

Montgomery House
https://www.amazon.com/dp/B073T1SVCN

Beautiful Fury
https://www.amazon.com/dp/B07B527N57

McCarthy Road
https://www.amazon.com/dp/B08NF5HYJG

Blind Date
https://www.amazon.com/dp/B08TPRZ5ZN

Heart's Love
https://www.amazon.com/dp/B09XBDK8LN

Check out the Epic Fantasy Adventure Available in Paperback, Ebook, and Audiobook

THE UNFADING LANDS

The Unfading Lands
https://www.amazon.com/dp/B00VKWKPES

Darkness Divided, Part Two in The Unfading Lands Series
https://www.amazon.com/dp/B015QFTAXG

Redemption Rising, Part Three in The Unfading Lands Series
https://www.amazon.com/dp/B01G5NYSEO

AND DiAMONDY THE BAD GUY

Katharine and her five-year-old son released Captain Cornfield and Diamondy the Bad Guy in November 2021. This new books series launched with great success and has brought Katharine's career full circle and back to children's literature for a co-author partnership with her son. She loves working on Captain Cornfield adventures and looks forward to book two releasing in 2022.

Captain Cornfield and Diamondy the Bad Guy: The Great Diamond Heist, Book One

https://www.amazon.com/dp/1735812579

Captain Cornfield and Diamondy the Bad Guy: The Dino Egg Disaster, Book Two
https://www.amazon.com/dp/B0B7QGTSFV

Subscribe to Katharine's Newsletter for news on upcoming releases and events!
https://www.katharinehamilton.com/subscribe.html

Find out more about Katharine and her works at:
www.katharinehamilton.com

Social Media is a great way to connect with Katharine. Check her out on the following:

Facebook: Katharine E. Hamilton
https://www.facebook.com/Katharine-E-Hamilton-282475125097433/

Instagram: @AuthorKatharine

Contact Katharine:
khamiltonauthor@gmail.com

ABOUT THE AUTHOR

Katharine started to read through her former paragraph she had written for this section and almost fell asleep. She also, upon reading about each of her book releases and their stats, had completely forgotten about two books in her repertoire. So, she put a handy list of all her titles at the beginning of this book, for the reader, but mostly for her own sake. Katharine is also writing this paragraph in the third person... which is weird, so I'll stop.

I love writing. I've been writing since 2008. I've fallen in love with my characters and absolutely adore talking about them as if they're real people. They are in some ways, and they've connected with people all over the world. I'm so grateful for that. And I appreciate everyone who takes the time to read about them.

I could write my credentials, my stats, and all that jazz again, but quite frankly, I don't want to bore you. So, I'll just say that I'm happy. I live on the Texas Coast, (no ranch living for now), and I have two awesome little fellas (ages six and two) who keep me running... literally. Though I also say a lot of, "Don't touch that." "Put that back." "Stop pretending to bite your brother." "Did you just lick that?"

Thankfully, I have a dreamboat cowboy of a husband who helps wrangle them with me. I still have my sassy, geriatric chihuahua, Tulip. She may be slowing down a bit, but she will still bite your finger off if you dare try to touch her... the sweetheart. And then Paws... our loveable, snuggle bug, who thinks she is the size of a chihuahua, but is definitely not.

That's me in a nutshell.

Thank you for reading my work.

I appreciate each and every one of you.

Oh, and Claron has now sold over 100,000 copies. Booyah!

And Graham is not far behind him.... Woooooooo!

Made in the USA
Columbia, SC
03 December 2024